BLACK LEATHER PANTS

Beth D. Carter

EROTIC ROMANCE

Siren Publishing, Inc.
www.SirenPublishing.com

A SIREN PUBLISHING BOOK
IMPRINT: Erotic Romance

BLACK LEATHER PANTS
Copyright © 2010 by Beth D. Carter

ISBN-10: 1-60601-536-2
ISBN-13: 978-1-60601-536-0

First Printing: February 2010

Cover design by Jinger Heaston
All cover art and logo copyright © 2010 by Siren Publishing, Inc.

Printed in the U.S.A.

PUBLISHER
Siren Publishing, Inc.
www.SirenPublishing.com

DEDICATION

For Lark, who lent me her name, her shoulder, her ear, and taught me her mad pool skills. My world is a much brighter place with you in it, my friend.

BLACK LEATHER PANTS

BETH D. CARTER
Copyright © 2010

Chapter 1

Penny lowered the visor and checked her eyes one more time. She thought she had done a good job hiding her sleepless night, though she knew her boss, Kiley, wouldn't be fooled for long. A skilled artist as well as a gallery owner, he would recognize the make-up job if she weren't careful.

She sighed. Oh well, she had done her best with Visine and cucumber eye gel to reduce the puffiness. If she could get through the next twelve hours without breaking down into a crying mess, she would be extremely proud of herself.

She flipped the visor up, grabbed her backpack purse from the passenger seat and opened the door on her twenty-year-old Volkswagen Beetle. The car had been a treasure to find, the first car she had ever bought with her own money. Its faded yellow color had once been so vibrant that Penny doubted it was the original color, but it suited her perfectly. She had black hair and a creamy complexion. Yellow was her natural foil. She loved color, art, and bringing it all together. It brought her to Los Angeles two years ago and working for Kiley Laurent at his gallery, Papillon. He had moved to California to pursue his own dream of being an art manager and gallery owner after a successful career as an artist and art critic in New York City.

Though his gallery was a huge success, mainly due to his ability to spot burgeoning talent, the upcoming show planned to be the ultimate make or break deal. He had landed a particularly outstanding new painter, an artist with a deft flare that hadn't been seen in art for years. Kiley had high hopes for the young man, Jedidiah Yuki, whose first exhibit would be held in two weeks. Both Penny and Kiley had been working long hours in the gallery to make sure all last minute problems that might arise would not.

Penny punched in her code to the back of the building and made her way up the stairs to the second floor. On the first floor, the gallery was a large and bright room with windows for walls. Her office was located upstairs next to Kiley's.

She paused outside the closed door, heard him moving around preparing for the day, and took a deep breath. Her nerves were shot. Her tears underneath the surface were ready to fall again at any moment. She curled her fingers into her palms and used her nails to inflict pain, pulling her emotions back from her broken heart.

"Good morning," she said cheerfully. She moved behind her desk and took several long minutes to put her backpack in a bottom desk drawer. She kept her face averted from Kiley as he walked up to her desk and sat in the chair facing her. He placed a mug of coffee on her desk.

This was the normal routine of their day. They relaxed for the first few minutes, catching up what they should accomplish for the day, what Kiley hoped before the reality of what would probably happen.

"Jed called me at four this morning," he grunted as he blew on his hot shot of morning caffeine.

"Anything wrong?"

"He had a brainstorm. He thought it would be a wonderful idea to serve wiener dogs as the hors d'oeuvre instead of caviar. He said it would make the atmosphere more homey."

Penny reached for her mug, making sure to keep her eyes averted. "So we're aiming for country bumpkin instead of artiste."

"*Imbécile*. I told him if he ever called me at four in the morning again I'd give him a black eye."

She smiled, having a hard time picturing Kiley as a brute. He stood a little taller than average, topping her own five foot five by a good five inches, with a body lean and muscular in that Gentleman GQ way. He would have fit in perfectly as a model for some Calvin Klein underwear ad. His face all sculptured bone and sharp angles. She thought the term metrosexual fit him perfectly.

Even today, on a casual day of preparation, he dressed in tight-fitting leather pants, a torso-hugging sweater to complement his physique and trendy sandals on his feet. On most men the outfit would probably sit uneasily, but on Kiley it was downright sinful.

Penny had many dirty thoughts about her boss. Mainly alone in her bed late at night, her fingers and trusty vibrator working their magic, but she decided not to think along those lines right then.

"Have you heard a single thing I've said?" Kiley asked.

Penny blinked and snapped her gaze to his. She instantly saw the annoyance in his royal blue eyes fade into concern.

"What's the matter?" he asked.

"Nothing." She sighed. She sat her cup down and folded her hands together to lean her forehead against them. "Everything. Stu broke up with me last night. I found him with a box packing up all his things at my apartment last night when I got home."

"Wasn't even going to wait until after work?"

She sighed and sat back to look at him. "That was kinda the problem. My work and you."

"Me?" he asked in a surprised tone.

She nodded. "He accused me of being too devoted to you and not to him."

Kiley snorted. "Typical male answer when the girl doesn't bend over backward tying to placate."

"I guess so. It hurt, but not as much as him telling me I wasn't sexy enough to keep his interest."

Kiley muttered something French under his breath. "What does that mean?"

"He pointed out the fact that I wear sweats at night instead of negligees. He didn't like that I always wore jeans and not dresses. I told him he watches too many *Charmed* reruns. He adores Alyssa Milano."

Kiley smiled at that. He stood and pushed back a few strands of her hair with his fingers. "Come here." He walked around the desk and pulled her into his arms, hugging her tightly to his chest.

His chest was quite nice. In fact, his whole body was nice. This was the first time she had been this close to him, held tightly in arms that were strong and comforting. His scent tickled her nose, an elusive combination of aftershave and sweet male that rolled over her. He was warm, just the right height for her to let her head rest in between his pecs. And what fine, nicely formed pecs she mused.

"I like your look," he said. He said something else, but she didn't really hear it. She was content to let the rumble of his sounds wash over.

One arm curled around the middle of her back, but the other hand rested on her nape, and chill bumps started to slide over her spine. His breath brushed over the tips of her ears, disturbing the fine hair around them, causing a strange heating sensation in her belly.

He pulled back and winked down at her before turning to make his way back to his own office. Penny watched his ass as he walked away with deep appreciation. It should be illegal how he filled out a pair of black leather pants.

Her mind wandered for a moment. She let herself wonder what it would be like to run her hands over that tightly encased rear, up his firm backside to slide over perfected muscles. Her palm itched to feel leather, gliding over it as she nipped and licked her way over his skin, inch by inch. She would give that tight ass a good slap to make him moan.

The imaginary slap ringing through, her ears jerked her back to the present. Penny shook her head and argued with her heart to slow down. Work. That was the best thing for her now. She obviously had way too much distraction on her mind.

She flipped on her computer and picked up her mug, finishing off the coffee now that it had cooled enough not to burn her taste buds. She logged onto the Internet and brought up her email, noticing mostly junk mail and a couple from Jed Yuki. She opened them and had to smile. He was trying to sell her to the idea of wiener dogs. She gave a mental thanks to whatever powers that be he didn't have her number.

She replied to the few emails she needed to, collected the mail and organized it. The day rolled on.

For a Monday it was actually boring, which was good for her frame of mind. She wasn't really up to the challenge of sorting out problems or dealing with clients. As much as she loved art, artists could be pains to deal with. At some point she sent a mental thanks to Stu that he picked a Sunday night for breaking up with her. If it had to be, this was the best time.

She snorted at the thought. Leave it to her to try to rationalize heartbreak. Perhaps that was her problem, the overanalyzing of everything. She supposed it could be blamed on her art background, the looking for meaning in everything. She found it hard to let a cigar be a cigar.

Around lunchtime Kiley came out of his office. He had spent the morning on the phone soliciting the upcoming show, roving around his office with the headpiece attached to his belt. She could see the little monitor hooked on his belt loop and wondered how one man could be so downright sexy.

She gave him an overly bright smile.

He frowned. "Want to go out for some sushi?"

Her smile slipped a bit. "I'm not very hungry. I'm afraid I wouldn't do justice to your credit card."

He looked at her desk. "It would do you good to eat something, go outside."

"I'm just not up to it."

"*Merde*! The prick wasn't worth it," he snapped at her. He stopped and half turned away, running a tanned hand through his blond streaked hair. "Sorry, that came out a bit too harsh."

She gazed at him, anger slowly building. "You're right. He isn't worth it. I know that and I'll get past it, but right now I don't feel like doing anything. Being rejected is cruel."

He gave a sympathetic smile.

"Don't smile like that."

He lost the look.

Her voice started to rise. "I bet you've no idea what it feels like to be rejected, to be belittled. I bet no woman has ever turned you down."

Now he frowned. "Wait a minute—"

"Oh, just go on with your sushi," she jumped to her feet. "I have to go to the bathroom."

Her breaking point had just hit. The pent- up tears she had repressed all day suddenly decided they needed to fall. She ran to the bathroom and locked the door behind her. Once she was safely behind it, tucked securely away where Kiley couldn't see her, all happy fabrication died. Sobs took over and she slid down the wall, her arms hugging around her body as she came to sit on the tiled floor.

She was so angry she could barely control the flood of tears. She was angry over Stu's words, angry at the inadequacy he made her feel, and angry that she wasn't more angry at his breaking up with her. His words had hurt, yes, but her heart remained unbroken.

One minute turned to two and finally into ten. When the storm subsided, she felt immensely better. Relieved, and actually lighter, as if years had been erased from her mind and baggage gone.

She went to the sink where her reflection made her wish she could crawl under a rock and hide for the next hundred years. Her make-up was shot. Even the waterproof mascara couldn't hold up to the rubbing that she had given her eyes. All her eyeshadow was gone with black streaks from her eyeliner running down her cheeks like a clown's face.

And her eyes were red again. Great. It was a good thing Kiley knew she didn't drink all that much else he'd think she was a lush.

Penny ran the hot water from the faucet and used the hand soap to wash her face. The heat against her puffy skin felt like heaven. Over and over she brought the hot water to her face and let it melt away her crying ordeal.

When she was done, she dried her face with hand towels and studied herself in the brightly-lit mirror. Her short black hair was damp around the edges, but overall she thought she looked okay. Well enough now to face the rest of the day, sans make-up.

She unlocked the bathroom door, shut off the light and made her way back to her desk. Kiley was nowhere to be seen, and she figured he probably went out for his lunch. Now, after her release of pent-up emotion and energy, she regretted turning down his offer. There was nothing like a good cry to make one's stomach rumble.

An hour later, after munching on some crackers she found in the bottom of one of her desk drawers, Kiley walked back in. He came to a halt when he saw her.

"Are you all right?"

She gave him a weary smile. "I am now. I'm sorry about that whole scene."

He held up a hand and walked to stand in front of her desk. "I shouldn't have said what I said. I just...don't like to see you so upset."

"I'm fine now." She handed him a couple of messages. "Did you enjoy your sushi?"

"I didn't eat," he told her as he skimmed through the notes. "I couldn't." He sighed. "I met with George Ralkin this afternoon. He wants to pull out his backing on Yuki's show."

"What? He can't do that. We have a contract."

"I know. I reminded him of that and he reminded me that bad publicity had a higher cost than lawyer fees."

"What are we going to do?"

"We are going to work through this evening to find a suitable replacement."

She sighed and held up a delivery menu. "Would you like Thai this evening?"

* * * *

She moved away from her desk and into his office, the phones ringing one call after another. This part of the job she didn't much care for. She realized past the paint and the masterpieces it could create, art was a business, and that to a gallery owner it became all about funding, backing, and having the very prominent attend. Without critics praising it, modern art would just be a market for sidewalk sales. Penny knew Kiley's world had been that once. He had often commented how he wanted, actually needed to go one step further...and Penny stood right there beside him. Together, they would bring the world to focus on one unbelievable painter.

Art would become divinity, but only if they could get it all organized. This was the last week to cement all the financial details. Next week they would be arranging pieces in the gallery.

At seven Penny had their dinner delivered, and they took a break to enjoy the food. The day wound down and both sat on the floor, their backs propped against the couch. Between them sat several assorted cardboard cartons of rice, noodles and appetizers.

She used her chopsticks to scoop a large shrimp into her mouth. "Mmm, I'd stay here late any night late to eat this."

He leaned over and looked in her box, using his own chopsticks to grab a mushroom. "I could do without the phone tag marathon."

She swallowed and nodded, smiling at him. "Hmm, I think you secretly enjoy days like today. Keeps you on your toes."

"Shush, you'll give away all my trade secrets."

She took another bite and looked down at her bare feet, her smile turning into a frown. She had left her Nikes at Stu's house along with one of her Enya CDs. Damn. The Nikes she could do without, Enya, no way.

"What is it?" Kiley asked, breaking into her thoughts.

"I just remembered my stuff left over Stu's house. Crap." She looked down at the empty Thai box in her hand, not remembering having taken the last bite. She threw it in the wastebasket.

"I'll go with you if you want me to," he offered quietly.

She blew out a sigh. "My knight in shining armor."

"Well, in any case, a knight with...." He leaned over to his mini-bar, sliding open the bottom shelf and pulling out a bottle. "An exceptionally magnificent vintage German Riesling."

Penny laughed, but jumped to her feet to grab two glasses. He opened the bottle as she held both glasses up. He filled each up full.

"Trying to get me drunk?" she quipped as she eyed the rim of her glass.

He answered with ease. "Not at all. I just thought you could use a bit of relaxing."

They toasted carefully and took a sip, impressed with the flavor. Kiley was the kind of man who would know only the best, would drink only the best. He wasn't the type of man who would ever let someone break his heart and cry for the entire world to see.

"What are you thinking?"

"I'm so glad you didn't say 'penny for your thoughts'."

He smiled.

She sighed and took a very large swig of wine. She ignored his raised eyebrows. "I was thinking of you."

"Me?" He sounded very surprised.

"I wish I had your polish, your flair. You're the type of man who breaks hearts, not the type of person who gets one broken."

"Now that's just plain silly."

She sighed and took another deep sip of wine before holding out her glass to get it topped. She ignored the fact he only gave her half a glass. "Is it? Just look at you. I bet you've never been hurt."

"Not true."

She narrowed her eyes as she judged him. "You've been in love?"

He didn't look at her. He kept his eyes on his wine as he swirled it in his glass. "Yes. Of course."

"Art doesn't count. I meant people."

He smiled. "So did I."

This was a side of Kiley she had never seen in the year she worked with him, and she thought she'd seen every mood he had from funny, serious, angry, disgusted, to even sick and whiny. But lovelorn?

"Who was she?"

He took a sip of wine and sat his glass on the table to his right. "Someone I don't want to talk about. Now, enough wine for you, give me your glass."

"No." She held it way from his outstretched hand. "I'm not done."

"You've had more wine in the past few minutes than I've ever seen you drink. I think it would be wise if you gave me the glass."

"No." In defiance she took another large swallow.

"Penny," he warned. He reached over her and then stopped suddenly. She realized their lips were mere inches apart

She froze, her eyes locked onto his. She could feel his warm breath mingle with hers, could taste the intoxicating scent of sweet wine as it washed over. It sent her heart pounding and the blood rushing through her veins.

His blue eyes sharpened and they dropped down to her lips. She saw that he watched intently as she licked them with her tongue. With a groan he covered her lips with his own.

Heart thundering, Penny barely thought as she managed to find the other table to set her wine glass down. She didn't even hesitate as she encircled his neck with her arms.

It was madness. All thoughts ended. She existed on pure pleasure. Kiley's tongue slid into her mouth, twined with hers, danced, jolting a salacious moan from her. He explored each hidden corner. In and out he plunged, sweeping aside any doubt that this was exactly where she needed to be at this moment. She was on fire from his kiss alone. His left hand came up to hold her head immobile while his right hand swept around her rib cage to pull her closer to his chest.

She had no conscious thought to go anywhere as the wine swimming through her head heated the fire in her blood. Her hands moved up to capture his face.

He groaned again deep in his throat and got to his knees, pulling her with him until she knelt in between his open thighs. As he kept kissing her deeper, hotter, wetter, she used the opportunity to run her hand down his chest and over the smooth line of his rear encased in the tight leather, not quite believing she had been given the opportunity to test out her fantasy.

The leather burned her hand and added fuel to the heat inside her own body. At the gentle touch, Kiley exploded into a frenzy. He pulled his lips from hers to run them down her neck. He found her pulse throbbing below the surface and gave a gentle suck on it. He licked and sucked, using tongue and teeth in ways that drove her deeper under his spell.

The world disappeared around them. Kiley quickly started unbuttoning her shirt, working his way down her chest with each inch revealed.

She let him. Penny leaned back and let him feast upon her flesh as he pulled the material aside and her bra melted off. He took one darkened nipple into his mouth, causing Penny to arch her back with a mewling sound, and began teasing the mound with gentle flicks. As he sucked and tugged, kneading with one hand, his other hand started to tease its way down her backside, over her butt and between her legs. He found her slit encased in her jeans, and made sweeping presses through the thick material, alternating the pressure with light and heavy strokes.

At that moment the wine hit her. All her inhibitions, if she had any remaining, simply vanished and she reacted on pure lust. She fell back, he with her, and her hands started tearing at his clothing.

His sweater pealed off and she delighted in exploring every inch of smooth, hairless skin. Her fingers undid the button of his pants and pulled down the zipper, slipping her hands inside and pushing the leather off his rear. Penny sank her nails into his ass, giving his flesh a smart slap.

He pulled back from her nipple and gazed down at her in sinful arousal. "You think I've been naughty?"

"A very bad boy," she panted.

He cast her a wicked grin and bent to capture her mouth again. His tongue slipped deep into her mouth as he unbuttoned her jeans. He slipped his fingers inside, finding the nub drenched in moisture. With alternating sweeps of pressure, he rubbed her clit, making her gasp and clench as desire pulsed through her.

"You're so wet," he muttered. They finished undressing, tossing garments aside in haste. Kiley settled between her thighs, rocking, banging his cock against her slit. His hands moved down her body, caressing her leg until he grabbed her knee and brought her leg up to grip him around his hip. He moved his hand inward, grasping her thighs.

"Open for me," he whispered, demandingly, pushing her legs open wide. As she lay there, staring at him through half closed eyes, Kiley trailed his middle finger toward her, past the dark curls to rub her lightly. He didn't need to go in any farther. Penny arched her back from the floor with a gasp, her eyes flying open to meet his.

"Ah," he murmured, rubbing again, using her slickness to coat his finger. Feather light caresses, faster, harder, over and over. Her body coiled, wound tight, all she could do was balance for a moment on the precipice and then fall.

"Unhh," she moaned as the orgasm crashed over her.

Kiley moved up as she rode the crest, lifting her head with one hand to kiss her. His other hand still teased her sex as he settled in between her open thighs. His fingers held open her lips as he guided himself right up to her, his cock giving one nudge as if found its home. Unable to hold back, he thrust forward, burying himself completely.

He moaned and paused, dropping his head and resting it on her shoulder. "Ah," he rasped. *"Viens m'enculer,* Penny….*Sacrebleu."*

She curved her body up, lifting her legs to hug around him as she crushed herself fully against him. She felt his heart thunder next to her own, her nipples digging like pebbles. She squeezed him with her walls, gently, letting him know she felt him deep inside. He moaned again and gave a fluid jerk with his hips.

Her body began to shiver in pure lust. "Fuck me, Kiley," she moaned. "Faster."

He pushed himself up on his elbows and his mouth sought hers as he moved again. At first he rocked gently, picking up speed as the ride continued. Her cunt made wet, slurping noises as he hammered into her, stretching her pussy lips with gasps of pleasure. In response she grabbed him with her vaginal walls, sucking him in more deeply and squeezing tight.

"*Mon Dieu,*" he muttered in pleasure-pain. "It's so hot, you're so fucking hot. I wanted this to last…I can't..." He gasped. "I can't hold back."

"Don't," she whispered back. "Please don't. Come with me."

His hips jerked once, twice, and his breath came in a hiss as the crest broke over him. He stiffened as his release pulsed through her, the hot core of him pushing her over the edge seconds later. He collapsed on her, panting and sweaty. She relished it, hugging him even as her own heart beat out of control from the tiny shocks of electricity that still soared deep within her.

And then the phone rang.

"Damn it!" Kiley stretched out an unsteady hand to grab the hand unit phone. "Papillon Gallery," he uttered harshly into the mouthpiece.

Penny lay on her back, panting, as reality started to seep in. *Oh...my...god....* What had she done? She had just slept with her boss. Well, no, not slept. Sex. She just had sex with her boss. Sex. With Kiley. Mind-blowing, out-of-this-world, unbelievable sex. With Kiley. Her boss. *Oh...my...god....*

"Calm down, Jed," Kiley said into the phone. He turned and gave her an apologetic shrug. "Listen to me. This has no reflection on you as an artist...."

He turned his back on her, moving to his desk, heedless of being naked. She watched his ass, the same ass she had admired earlier when it was clothed in leather, never dreaming she would ever see it out of the leather. She had just had sex with her boss. Like, what clichéd romance novel had she just experienced?

Oh...my...god....

She took a steady breath and tried to relax her brain. All right, it had to be the wine. Blame it on the wine. For some reason alcohol went right to her pleasure center and made her forget decent behavior.

Would Kiley believe the wine excuse?

Oh...my...god....

This was a nightmare. She looked again at Kiley and his back turned as he talked Jed Yuki out of one crisis or another. Though he moaned and groaned about it, he had the type of voice and the hypnotic presence that could calm anyone.

She just had sex with her boss. What was she supposed to do now?

Penny grabbed her clothes. The first thing she wasn't going to do was lie there naked. She stood, ignoring the delicious feeling of her body in spent languor, and hurriedly dressed. The wetness between her thighs she would deal with later.

Not looking at Kiley as he continued to talk on the phone, she rushed out of the office and over to her desk. She grabbed her backpack purse and pulled out her keys. If there ever was a time she needed for introspection, now was the time.

She paused on her way out the main door and looked back at Kiley's office. Things were different now, forever changed. Even if they were able to move past this she doubted she'd be able to forget.

How could she possibly work with him now?

Chapter 2

When she saw her beat up old Beetle she gave a mental sigh of relief. Comfort and sanity, as well as her escape method. She unlocked the door, slid behind the wheel and cranked the engine.

Dead. Nothing. Not even a semblance of trying to hold onto life. The alternator didn't even turn over.

"No," she muttered, despair washing through her. She turned the key again. No life whatsoever. "Don't do this to me. Not today, please not now."

The prayer went unanswered. The little car died. It had always been temperamental, and she knew life in it was precious. But now, facing the reality of walking back into the office and facing a naked Kiley, she realized how utterly horrible the prospect of not having transportation.

She sat for a moment as options swirled through her head. She had already ruled out going back into work, which left out a taxi, or perhaps a bus. There wasn't a subway system in Los Angeles, at least one that didn't extend out toward Century City, so that left the bus route.

Without another wasted thought, she jumped out of her car and locked the door behind her. She looked around the parking lot, knowing it would be safe for the night. Tomorrow she would deal with it and whatever services she would have to do to get it towed to a garage.

Tonight, however, she just wanted to sleep. And a bath. A cool stickiness ran between her thighs and kept reminding her that she had, perhaps, committed the worst possible sin an assistant could commit.

She pulled her backpack tighter to her chest and started walking. The bus stop wasn't too far away, at the corner of the next major intersection. Even in Los Angeles the night wasn't too dark. She had streetlights to help her navigate.

What a day, to go from being dumped to sleeping with the boss. Where to take that? What to say when she saw him tomorrow? Kiley Laurent was an amazing man, a man who made other men look bad. Bold, stylish, confident and debonair, women turned their heads to watch him walk down the street. She had seen several women he had dated and none of them looked like Penny Varlet, small town girl from Missouri. If she appeared in public on his arm, people would wonder what brain fever he suffered from.

She sighed. What absolute morose thoughts, and how absurd. Never had Kiley ever shown an ounce of pettiness over his looks. He wasn't self-centered or egotistical, well except when it came to art, his one area of vanity.

As she walked along busy Santa Monica Boulevard, lost in thoughts, a honking came from behind her. Lights flashed. She stopped and looked, and noticed Kiley's blue BMW Z-3 pull up to the curb. He rolled down the passenger window.

"Get in," he said harshly.

Truthfully, she didn't really feel like taking the bus all the way into the Valley, especially since she didn't know which bus to take. She stepped to the passenger side and opened the door, and slid into the little two-seater. The leather seats reminded her of the leather pants that were back on his body and she stifled a groan.

"I saw your car and you were nowhere around. Why the hell are you walking?"

"My car wouldn't start."

He didn't say anything as he drove down Santa Monica Boulevard until the sign for the 405 Freeway came up. He maneuvered the tiny car through the traffic and eased onto the still heavily congested highway. No matter what time of day the 405 from Wilshire

Boulevard, over the pass, to where the Ventura Freeway met, was always congested. Newcomers to the area gave it the nickname The Parking Lot and locals usually tried to find alternate routes over the mountain and into the Valley.

"I should have taken Sepulveda," Kiley muttered. He looked in his rearview mirror before shifting gears to maneuver into the fast lane.

"That's just as bad," she said staring out the passenger window where she could see the parallel road. Tonight it was just as crowded as the 405.

"Why did you leave?" he asked very softly, keeping his eyes on the road.

"I thought it best."

He hesitated. "I didn't use protection."

She blinked. "Do you have something I should be concerned about?"

"No."

"Neither do I. And I'm on the pill."

"Penny...."

"Do we have to discuss this now?" She didn't think she could bear hearing him tell her how much a mistake tonight had been.

He didn't say anything, he just drove. An uncomfortable silence stretched between them, something that had never existed before, and it churned her stomach. At that moment, she would have given anything to take back the past hour.

It took them another twenty minutes to reach her tiny apartment in the Valley off Ventura Boulevard. She watched with passionless eyes as he curved up to the curb and shifted into neutral.

"I'll pick you up tomorrow morning," he muttered. "Six-thirty."

She nodded. "Thank you."

He acknowledged with his own nod.

It was the first time neither could say anything to each other and it was quite disheartening.

"Good night," she said and opened the car door.

"Penny," he called out. She leaned down and looked at him. His eyes were clouded, wary, before he finally shook his head. "Good night."

She had a funny feeling that wasn't what he wanted to say. She watched him drive off until his tail lights blurred with all the other tail lights, only then making her way up to the security box and hitting her entry code. The door clicked and she made her way to her apartment on the top floor. Long ago when she moved in, she decided to get on the top because in the event of an earthquake, she didn't want to be buried in the bottom.

What a warped way of thinking.

She flicked on the overhead light and saw she had several messages on her machine. The first from her mother calling to tell her some meaningless matter on the heat wave seeping over the central part of the United States. Next her friend Lark left a message wanting to know if she wanted to hit a movie on the weekend. The third and last from Kiley demanding to know where she was. Obvious that call had been sent before he had found her walking. She could hear the whirl of his engine through the cell phone recorded on the machine.

How odd to hear that message and know it had been right after they made love...er, had sex. Did one have to be in love to make love? And if she thought of it as making love, did that mean she thought of Kiley as more than just her boss?

The phone rang at that moment, startling her. She picked up her receiver. "Hello?" For some reason hoping to hear Kiley's voice.

"Finally, you're home," Lark declared. "I've been trying to reach you for ages. Honestly, girl, get a cell phone."

Penny smiled. "Yeah yeah, soon. I promise."

"You've been working?" Lark asked her. In the background Penny could here traffic.

"Yeah."

There must have been something in that one word to alert Lark all was not well. "What happened? Are you okay?"

"I'm fine...except...you'll never believe this, Lark, I..." She bit her lip.

"You what?"

"I had...sex...with Kiley."

Silence. Then, "You're kidding! No way! Penny? No way, right?"

"Too right. I can't believe it happened. We'd been working late, sitting around and...oh, did I tell you Stu dumped me?"

"Whoa, Stu dumped you and you slept with your boss. Anything else?"

"My car died."

"You're three for three now, Pen. When it rains, it pours."

Penny groaned.

"Still, I don't blame you. Kiley Laurent is one mega hunk. I just can't believe it took you a year to do the nasty with him."

"Lark," Penny reproached.

"Penny," she countered in the same tone of voice. "Come on, like you haven't fantasized about him before in a panty wetter."

"Shush, you foul mouthed friend. My boyfriend just broke up with me!"

"And I can tell you're really broken up about that." The sound of a huff came through loud and clear. "As if that loud-mouthed racist had ever been any threat to your heart."

"He liked you, really."

"Yeah, he liked calling me his 'brown sugar babe' whenever you weren't around. I'm glad he dumped you."

"Lark!"

"You know what I mean. I'm sorry you're hurt and all, but truthfully, is your heart really broken?"

Penny sighed. "What am I going to do? I have to face Kiley tomorrow morning."

"You are going to fill that tub of yours, splash some of that scented salts I gave you for your birthday in it, soak and wash your hair and then hit the sheets and dream of the golden Adonis with sucky little noises to guide to you sleep. Tomorrow, attack him and have wild passionate sex again."

"You are incorrigible."

Lark chuckled. "No, just romantic. I've never met two people so in tune with each other."

"Hmm. Don't you think he's too...chic for me? Stu is more my speed."

"Girl, get that mentality out of your head right now. I'd slap you if I were there. You liked Stu because he came from BFE just like you. But you are not some hick. You are beautiful and you are wild!" She drew out the word 'wild' as if it had two syllables. "Besides, I bet it was more like, I'm getting too old to keep looking for someone to love me. Honey, hit yourself for me. Good girl. Now repeat after me: I am worthy, I am worthy."

"I think you've been watching *Wayne's World* again."

Lark chuckled. "Possibly. Anyway, gotta run. Want to get together this weekend?"

"Definitely. Saturday or Sunday?"

"Sunday. I'll probably be recovering from my weekly hangover on Saturday. I'll pick you up at noon. *Ciao*!"

She rang off without waiting for replay. Penny smiled as she hung up the phone. Lark was like that. They met soon after Penny moved to Los Angeles, both interviewing with Kiley for the secretary/assistant position. They had been waiting together, started chatting, and hit it off fabulously. Even though Penny got the position, Lark declared the friendship a great trade.

If there was one thing Lark was right about, it was the fact that she didn't miss Stu as much as she should, if she had truly loved him. Really, what hurt the most was his rebuff and utter indifference to her as a person. Kiley had said he liked her just the way she was...

Oh, Kiley again.

Penny sighed and made her way into the bathroom. It always came back to him.

Chapter 3

She decided to wear yellow the next morning. Not only did it best suit her coloring and brought out her deep brown eyes, but it lent a silent nod of support for her dead car. She picked a yellow headband and pushed her hair back out of her face. Just the way she liked it.

Five minutes before six-thirty she waited in the lobby for Kiley to show up. Always on time, he was one of those types of people who thought promptness was next to Godliness.

She had no idea what to say to him. Certainly nothing about what had happened yesterday. Though it had been one of the most awesome, toe-curling moments of her life, she wouldn't be able to bare it if he were to start making excuses about it. It would kill her if he had to start avoiding her, or worse, feel the need to fire her. Her job was important to her, but more than that, Kiley was everything.

Penny frowned as she saw his BMW pull up outside the curb, exactly on time. When had Kiley gone from being just her boss to *everything*?

"What's wrong today?" he asked her warily as she slid into the passenger seat.

She grabbed her seat belt, doing her best to stay busy, but appear as if she wasn't trying to stay busy. "Nothing, why?"

"You're frowning."

"I am?" She mentally smoothed the frown lines between her eyes. "Just thinking before you pulled up."

"About?"

"Oh...this and that."

She saw his mouth tighten from the brush-off tone, and that conversation became the precedent for the rest of the day.

They rode the rest of the way in silence to the office, where Kiley parked in front as he tended to do. He unlocked the front door and shut off the silent alarm that consisted of a motion detector and invisible laser beams, a la James Bond. Penny always thought those types of sensors only existed in the movies, and was completely amazed when she saw them demonstrated. An aerosol can, sprayed at the right angle, really did reveal the laser beams. She discovered during the installment demonstration powered deodorant worked best.

They climbed the side stairs to the second floor where he unlocked the office door. The room was chilly since their climate control was set on economy, so Penny moved to turn it up a few degrees.

Kiley went into his office and shut the door. He didn't offer to make coffee, nor did he look inclined to. She left the office to go to the little kitchenette down the hall, plugging in the coffee maker and setting it up. She added an extra scoop of grounds into the filter.

One of the reasons why Kiley always insisted he make the coffee was because he thought her version too watery. She swore she used the same amount as he did, and in fact he watched her one morning make it, but it never held up under his taste test.

She supposed he would just have to get by with watery coffee today. She grabbed their mugs from the cabinet where the cleaning crew stored them and poured the brew into each. She added a hefty dose of cream to each mug. Neither one of them took sugar but they both loved the thick, rich cream. And none of that fat free or dairy free stuff for them, only the artery-clogging stuff would do.

She walked back to the office and put her mug down on her desk before heading to his door. She gave a light rap and walked in, expecting to see him on the phone or buried in some paperwork.

Instead he stood at his window that overlooked the gallery floor. The window was a tinted two-way mirror where he could see down, but no one could see up. His desk stood on the opposite side, facing the window. The couch and mini-bar located on the opposite side of the door. Though a small office, it had been decorated tastefully in tones of sand and cinnamon, rich colors that made the inhabitants feel at ease.

Penny did her best to keep her eyes clear of the couch, as it did not inspire peace and tranquility at the moment. She made a beeline for his desk, placing the mug of coffee down before turning to leave just as quickly.

"Do you have a mechanic?"

She paused, one hand on the doorknob. She looked at him, and he half turned to look back. He was dressed in faded green pants that reminded her of parachutes, with zippers and ties, and a black, long-sleeved, skintight stretch top that rested right at his navel. The dark color accentuated his blond hair and the defined angles of his cheekbones. She swallowed hard. Truly, the man should be branded a lethal weapon, because he was killing her. "No. I plan on calling around to find the best quotes."

He pulled out his wallet from his back pocket. He flipped it open and pulled at a business card, passing it to her. "This is a friend of mine. I wouldn't trust my car to anyone but him. Call him. He'll give you a fair break."

She looked down at the card. Francois Reliquet. "He's French?"

"His parents are friends of my parents. He moved here several years ago from Paris."

Penny nodded. "Thanks, Kiley."

He gave her a dark, brooding smile and turned back to the window. "I'll be mostly in the gallery today supervising the arriving crates and touching up the background plates."

She left his office and headed out to her car on the off chance, cross-your-fingers luck that last night was a fluke. As she approached the little Beetle, she saw a note under one of her window wipers. She yanked it open and read quickly: *I saw you working late tonight. I'll be by tomorrow to drop off your stuff. Stu.*

Terrific, exactly what she didn't need today. She balled up the note and stuck it in the front pocket of her jeans to throw away when she passed a trashcan. She unlocked her door and slid in.

The key turned once, twice, and on the third motionless crank Penny caved in to defeat. Time to call Francois, the French friend.

Kiley actually held dual citizenship, French and American, though he preferred life in the States. He was born in Paris, maintained an apartment there, and always went back on vacations to visit his parents. He obtained his degree in Art History in France before switching over to study in New York City. His father had once been the curator of the Louvre, and his mother a patron of several other notable French museums. The love of art cultivated in his blood from birth, but his interest lay in the discovery of the next Picasso or Monet, and it was a passion she shared.

Though his native language was French, she had only heard him speaking it over the phone, and loved the way it rolled off his tongue. *Oh, definitely don't think of his tongue.* She still had quivers in her belly from that tongue.

The morning rolled by, and just as Kiley had told her, he went into the gallery and stayed there. In between calling Francois and trying to find a way home that night, she had her work to finish. The programs came in that day with a typo on them, so there wasn't a moment when the phone wasn't glued to her ear.

She didn't see Kiley at all, and had a funny feeling he decided to avoid her. It made her sad to think about.

At around two in the afternoon, she took a much needed bathroom break. In the mirror she found a vastly improved reflection from the day before. No red, puffy eyes, no morbid lines of make-up streaking her face. She looked as she always looked, and glad about it, considering Stu was going to make an appearance.

Muffled voices infiltrated through the hallway as she made her way back to her desk. Her mind looking forward to ordering some Italian delivery on the company's pay time, she startled when she heard her name.

Curious, she went to the door that separated the gallery from the upstairs and opened it. Stu stood there, at the bottom of the stairs with a box in his hands. Kiley stood next to him, hands balled, a sneer lifting one corner of his mouth. Both looked ready to beat the other senseless.

"What's going on?" she asked casually as she made her way down the stairs. Funny, looking at Stu produced no outstanding, devastating emotions, only a flat regret that she had wasted five months on the jerk.

"I was just telling Steve here...."

"Stu," Stu corrected.

"Whatever...that he could leave the box with me."

"Absolutely correct," she agreed. "But since I'm here now, thanks for this." She pulled out her Enya CD she had missed.

"You can play that upstairs if you want," Kiley offered. "I'm not using my CD player."

"Great," she smiled. "A little Enya soothes the savage soul."

"I knew it." Stu sneered, looking back and forth at them.

"Knew what?" Penny shook her head.

Stu raised a hand and with a finger wagged it between her and Kiley. "You two. I knew it."

"Wait a minute—" her voice broke off as Kiley put his hand on her waist and stepped in close next to her. Too close...way too close. Her heartbeat instantly went into hyperdrive.

"You figured it all out, haven't you, Steve?"

"Stu. My name is Stu."

"Whatever. Thanks to your little Alyssa Milano fetish, Penny and I were finally able to truly discover the depth of feelings we have for one another." And then he leaned over and kissed her, right on the lips.

Penny thought she would faint right there.

Kiley pulled away to go to the door and held it open. "Thank you so much for saving me a trip of collecting her belongings. Now, if you would so kindly...."

He waved his hand in a grand gesture of making sure Stu took the hint and went away.

Stu shot one last sneer at Penny and left.

"What was that all about?" she huffed, placing her hands on her hips.

"You didn't actually want him to hang around, did you?"

"No. But you implied...a thing between us."

"There is a thing between us, Penny," he countered, his voice rising slightly. "Yesterday, up there," he pointed to where his office sat behind the mirror, "we...."

"I know what we did!" She held her hands up. Even though she knew they were alone in the gallery she looked around to be sure.

"Are you ashamed?" he demanded.

"Yes," she replied and raised a hand to squeeze the bridge of her nose. "No," she groaned. "I'm confused. We breached a protocol that's strictly taboo. You're my boss, for heaven's sake!"

He took her hand. "And I'm also your friend."

"Still?"

"Of course."

"And you won't fire me?"

He blinked. "Is that what you thought I'd do? Slam, bam, thank you ma'am, now get the hell out?" He made a reproachful sound between his teeth. "Get back to work, Varlet."

He let go of her hand and turned away, walking back amidst the background decorations and sketches he had drawn. She reached up with her right hand to scratch the back of her neck and turned with her box of goodies to head back upstairs.

She put the box on the floor by her desk and pushed it up against the wall. Again pulled out her Enya CD and walked into Kiley's office to grab his disk player. Minutes later she sat at her desk, head hung forward, eyes closed letting the soothing music to wash over her.

Her stomach grumbled. Eyes still closed, she lifted the phone and placed a quick order to the Italian restaurant, ordering spinach raviolis for her self and Kiley's usual, vegetable lasagna. He wasn't that adventurous about Italian and tended to stick with the one thing he knew he liked, while she could eat it every day.

As soon as she hung up the phone it rang again. So much for the lunch reprieve.

"Papillon's," she murmured in her most pleasant, welcoming voice. She tried to inflict a hint of warmth in her tone. Lark had once told her she sounded like a 1-900 calling center and Penny had wondered for days how Lark had known what 1-900 girls sounded like.

"Ms. Varlet?"

"Speaking."

"This is Francois. *Bonjour*!"

"Oh, bonjour to you, Francois. I hope you have some good news."

"Well, good news and not the best news."

She pursed her lips. What did that mean? "Well, let's go with the good news first."

"Your little car is fixable. Do you know anything about engines?" He asked in his charming accent, all his 'i's ' sounding like 'e's'.

"No," she replied cautiously.

"No matter. Mainly, what has happened, lots of wires are really old and more or less disintegrated. The alternator is dead, and I found a small leak in the radiator, but I order you all new parts and it will be ready, good as new, in one week."

"Is that the not the best news part, it'll be ready in one week?"

"I am afraid *oui*, yes it is."

She held back a groan. "Well, Francois, call me in a week with wonderful news."

"Certainly. Would you like me to fax you the estimate I drew up? You sign and fax back to me."

She told him the fax number to the office.

"*Merci, au revoir!*" The line went dead.

"Yeah," she muttered as she hung up the phone. "Right back at ya."

Time to think. She had a week of having to get back and forth from the Valley to Century City, and a weekend of...well, nothing to do now, except for her outing with Lark on Sunday.

She pulled out her wallet from her backpack, finding her insurance card. She needed to make sure she didn't have rental car coverage. If she did, that would make all this a little easier.

Half an hour later Penny hung up the phone and leaned back in her chair, defeated. She had checked her bank account online, totaled the cost of a week of rental car fees, and choked on her spinach raviolis at the cost of repairs to her own car. She wanted to weep. There went her small savings and cushion, not to mention her plans for a nice vacation to some warm sandy beach.

She pushed her food away.

Kiley walked into the office and halted when he saw her rejected food. "Not good?"

"Not hungry," she corrected.

"What's the matter?"

She let out a deep, frustrated sigh and held up the faxed estimate. "Repair costs. I might as well sell a kidney on the black market to help pay for this."

Kiley took it from her, looking it over. "I can lend you money."

She held up a hand. "Thanks, but I got that end covered. You wouldn't happen to have another car lying around, would you? One you're not driving at the moment?"

He shook his head.

"Damn. Can you drive me to Rent-A-Wreck after work?"

"Ah, I see now. No rental car provision on your insurance?"

She shook her head. "But you can rest assured that will be revised as soon as I get my car back."

He put the fax back on her desk and sat down in the visitor chair. "No one can drive you to and from work?"

"With our hours? I'm here at seven in the morning and usually leave seven at night. Out of the two friends I have, Lark is a line producer for television so her schedule is just as off kilter as mine, and my other friend has two kids to look after." She rubbed her forehead. "I can always take the bus."

"You have another friend," he reminded her.

She stopped the rubbing and looked at him. "But you live on the other side of town, slightly impractical. I thank you, though."

"I wasn't suggesting I pick you up and drop you home every day. Why don't you come live with me for the week?"

Her jaw dropped. Literally. "Come again?"

Amusement touched his face. "I hope so," he teased, and laughed at her blush. "Listen, I have an extra bedroom in my condo with its own bathroom."

"Wow, I wasn't expecting that offer." Her brain kicked into fast forward. A week, with him...him only a wall away...would she be able to sleep at all knowing he would be so close? "Do you think that's wise after, er, you know?"

He ignored the question. "It makes sense. We work the same hours anyway. The condo is just a place to shower and rest and change our clothes." He shrugged.

Hmm, great idea. She had a mental freeze frame of him showering...suds running down each muscle with slick abandon, water sluicing over each curve.

"Penny?"

She started out of her daydream and picked up an envelope to fan herself with. "Yeah, all right."

Was it her imagination or did her voice come out as a squeak?

Chapter 4

She spent the rest of the day in a state of nervous agitation. How could she be expected to get any work done when, in mere hours, she would be going home with her sexy, gorgeous boss...whom she now knew in the biblical sense? God, who would have guessed a moment of weak madness would find her in such titillation?

The question, of course, is if given the chance, would she change what happened? Two days ago she had been completely content to date Stu, endure his pleasant kisses and ignore her boss's black leather pants. Yet something changed between Sunday night's tissue fest and Monday night's Thai food seduction. Could it be her awareness of Kiley as more than her boss kicked in when he had hugged her? That had been the first time there had ever been any type of physical content outside of the occasional hand or leg brushes...and man what a hug it had been. Then she had watched that fabulous ass walk away in those pants....

So, it all came down to the black leather pants. They had to be the cause of all this confusion she found herself in now. Damn them.

Penny picked up her phone, punching in Lark's number.

On the third ring she answered. "Hello?"

"I need you to buy me a book," Penny said without a greeting.

"All right," Lark answered readily. "What's the title?"

"Stupid things you do after you sleep with your boss."

The chuckle came in loud and clear. "I think I'd enjoy reading that book."

Penny groaned. "Not you, you have to be on my side."

"Well, what's the title of Chapter One?"

"Moving in with the boss."

"Holy shit! You're a fast worker."

Penny sighed. "It's only going to be for a week."

"You've doomed the relationship already?"

"No, no. My car won't be ready for a week, so Kiley offered to share his house with me so I can get to and from work. Since we have the same hours it's a purely logical, reasonable solution."

"You keep telling yourself that and you might just believe it. Me, I'll wear my boots 'cause it's getting thick in here."

"Oh shush," Penny reproached, and eyed Kiley as he walked back into the office. "I have to go. So Sunday pick me up at Kiley's house. Great. 'Bye."

She hung up and watched as he stopped in front of her desk. He held out some papers.

"What's this?" she asked, trying her best to ignore the sudden flare of passion that leapt up from her belly.

"The corrected program. It just came by courier. Look it over, double check it all again, and if everything is okay, call the printers up and run with it."

Penny nodded and took it from his hand. Their fingers brushed, electricity shot up arm. She did her best to not let it show.

But he stood there, watching her, so she finally looked up and caught his vivid blue gaze staring at her intently, as if he searched for something.

She cleared her throat. "Anything else?"

"We should talk about what happened."

"Um, now?"

"It doesn't have to be now, but soon." He ran a hand through his hair. "You can't think if you ignore it, it will go away."

"No, please." She held up a hand, halting him. "I know, Kiley. But...a lot has happened the past three days and I need time to digest it all."

He nodded. "Fair enough. Listen, I have to go out for the rest of the afternoon, but I'll be by here around five to pick you up. We'll go to your place so you can gather some things. Want to have dinner out?"

She smiled. "That'd be great."

So she had been granted a reprieve, at least for a few hours. The afternoon soon filled with calls, messages, deliveries and other monotonous tasks that managed to keep her fingers and her mind busy.

It was near five when the intercom to outside buzzed impatiently.

"Yes?" Penny asked absently.

"Delivery for a Ms. Fast Worker." Lark's voice came in loud and clear with a little giggle accenting it.

Penny buzzed her in and stood up to greet her friend. Lark was her own age, a little taller and about ten pounds thinner. Of mixed heritage, her mother white and her father black, Lark had inherited the most beautiful skin Penny had ever seen. Not just in color tone. Her complexion was flawless. Penny doubted Lark had ever had a pimple in her life.

Lark poked her head through the door. "Boss man here?"

Penny shook her head. "Meeting. Come in."

She held out a wrapped present. "Here, I brought you a gift."

Penny eyed it warily. Presents from Lark tended to embarrass. She took it and felt it...it felt like a book. What harm could a book do? At least it wasn't some see-through negligee or leather bra and matching zip-up panties.

She pulled the wrapping paper off and read the book title. "Wow, they actually have a book titled 'Mistakes After Sleeping With the Boss'."

Lark clapped her hands together in a happy gesture and laughed. "They have a book for everything! But look at Chapter One, go ahead." She helped Penny open the book.

Penny started reading. "Chapter One, A Quickie on the Desk." She looked at Lark. "Great. Thanks, just what I need. Ideas."

Lark continued to laugh as she plopped down in the chair in front of her desk. Well, it wasn't an actual plop. Lark never plopped. She was far too graceful and meticulous on how she moved. Penny suspected since Lark worked at a film studio, thus was in daily contact with the more glamorous side of Los Angeles. Truly, even the people who worked in the cafeterias at any movie studio seemed more glamorous, at least to those who fantasized about moving to Hollywood.

When Penny was in school she decided to move to Los Angeles and become a set designer or a background artist, somewhere that her love of art could flourish. But she forgot that she lacked the gumption to actually feel comfortable in pursuing such a life. In any case, she had found herself a great job doing exactly what she loved, and didn't think for a second she had sold out on the 'Hollywood stardom' job.

"So for Sunday there's a screening being held I thought we could go to." Lark named an upcoming movie that Penny had been waiting patiently to see.

"Great! I planned to go see that on opening night, but now I won't have to stand in any lines, or shell out any money."

Screenings were private showings held by the studio of the films that financed and released them. Reserved for critics and the people who had worked hard to bring the film together, all Lark had to do was put her name down, with a guest, and they would get to see before the rest of the world.

Truly, Lark not getting this job and landing one the next day at Paramount had been the best thing that ever happened to Penny. What a coup to have a friend with special accesses.

"So...when I pick you up on Sunday, are you going to be like, all gooey eyed and gaga?"

Penny, who had been flipping through the book, wrinkled her nose at her friend before tossing the book onto her desk. "I shall plead the fifth."

Lark snorted. "No fair. How about a bet?"

"A bet?"

"Say, if on Sunday, you can't shut up about the wonderful charms of Mister Frenchman, and I see little hearts shining from your eyes, you pay up. Twenty bucks."

"Twenty!"

Lark shrugged. "You have nothing to worry about if you can spend a week with him and not fall in love."

Penny sighed. "Love? I'm still trying to figure out why I jumped his bones over Thai food."

Lark laughed again and pointed over her shoulder. "Right in there?"

"I've been avoiding that room as much as possible."

"So...about the bet?"

"You know, I don't think I'm going to win, so I'll regretfully decline."

"Oh pooh," she pouted for a minute before brightening into a smile. "That must mean you must believe you are falling for him."

Penny picked up the book. "Chapter One."

"Yeah, but did you see Chapter Five?"

Penny opened to the table of contents and skimmed down. She groaned and read out loud, "Chapter Five, Moving In."

At that moment Kiley walked into the office. As he flashed a grin to Lark, Penny scrambled to hide the book.

Lark stood to kiss each cheek, the way a proper European says hello. Lark really loved customs. "I just stopped in to see my best girlfriend. I swear I didn't take her away from her duties."

He smiled ever so charmingly. "You are welcome anytime. Did Penny invite you to the opening?"

Lark turned and gave her a sour look. "No, she did not, you little rat."

"I planned on telling you." Even to Penny's ears the excuse sounded feeble.

"Yeah yeah. Sweetie, never say 'it's in the mail' to a producer." She smiled to show she wasn't upset before turning back to Kiley. "When is it, and is it black tie?"

"A week from Friday, and no, not black tie. Suit and tie."

Lark winked. "I have the perfect stunning little dress." Kiley laughed again. "Well, I'm off." She picked up her purse and leaned over to kiss Penny on the cheek. "I'll be calling you."

With a wave she left, leaving them both smiling.

"Ready?" Kiley asked her.

"Oh, I just have to close up."

He went into his office while she put the answering machine on, checked the fax paper for anything coming in at night, and straightened her desk as much as possible. After shuffling the same stack of mail back and forth for the fifth time she gave up. Stalling wasn't going to change anything. She shut down her computer, rose and grabbed her backpack purse before heading to Kiley's door and knocking on it.

"I'm ready."

Kiley, seated on the couch, nodded and placed his half-filled tumbler of what she knew to be brandy on the side table.

She watched how his black shirt stretched across the chest as he stood and hated the dryness that suddenly took over her mouth, suddenly very glad she didn't take Lark's bet.

She followed him outside and down the stairs to his car. He held open her door as she slid inside his BMW and watched as he walked around. The color, an electric blue, was a dead match for his eyes. The sports car was compact and sleek, every line smooth with a feeling of power and control vibrating through every rumble. Kiley was the type of man who did justice to the car, not the other way around. She had seen other people driving the same type BMW and they had seemed...effeminate.

Kiley was all man. And she should know.

Instead of taking the 405 like the previous night, he zipped over to 26th Street to hit San Vicente, turning onto Bundy until he hit Sunset Boulevard. This way proving to be easier to get onto Sepulveda Boulevard without the crunch of the freeways.

Kiley turned on his CD player and hit a few buttons before relaxing to the drive. A harsh drumbeat immediately filled the car.

"Who's this?" Penny asked.

"Nickleback."

"Oh." Clearly clueless, but trying hard to place the voice.

He glanced over to her. "You ever see the movie *Spiderman*?"

"The one with Tobey Maguire? Of course, what a great movie."

Her enthusiastic answer surprised him. "The lead singer from Nickleback sung the main song."

She listened for a moment. "Oh yeah, that's where I've heard him before. This guy has an amazing voice."

"What other movies do you like?"

"I like everything except horror. I don't like having nightmares, and my imagination works overtime."

He smiled. "Wait till you see my collection."

"What's your favorite all time move?" she asked, watching his profile.

His lips quirked to one side. "Of all time?"

"Of any category. I promise I won't make fun."

"Let's see...I would have to say *Zoolander*."

"Are you kidding?"

He chuckled. "Yes, but I do like that one. Mmmm, I tend to like independent films. I thought *Dead Man* with Johnny Depp was brilliant."

She nodded. "I liked that one too. I don't know if I have a single favorite. I like Kurosawa films. Foreign films. Of course, I also like good popcorn flicks that have no other purpose than escapism."

"Nothing wrong with escapism," he murmured, his eyes never leaving the road in front of him.

At her apartment he waited downstairs while she ran up to pack. She grabbed a small suitcase and threw in what she thought would be enough clothes, make-up, face wash, her anti-aging night cream, and toothbrush.

She walked out the door and slid back into the car fifteen minutes later. "Dinner?" she asked.

"What would you like?"

"Sushi, since I missed out on it yesterday."

"There's actually a great place near my condo. Hold on." He made the turn and off they went.

Chapter 5

Even the sushi bar he took her to reflected his metrosexual groove. Very swank and suave, the sushi maker guys greeted him in Japanese, to which he responded hello in their language.

He led her away from the circular bar to a table and held out her chair like a perfect gentleman. As he took his own seat, he grabbed the order sheet, marking off various items. He didn't ask her what she wanted. They had eaten sushi together enough times that he knew exactly what her palate enjoyed.

"There is a question I've always wanted to ask you," she murmured, watching him give the order sheet to the waitress, a lovely Japanese girl who smiled friendly at Kiley in recognition.

"And two iced green teas," he said with a polite smile before turning back to Penny. "Uh oh." He grinned. "All right, go ahead."

"Where do you get your clothes?"

He blinked. "My clothes? Well, Paris. I do all my shopping there, I like the trends. Why? Don't like them?"

"No, it's not that." She shook her head. "I have always loved your style. Stylish, hip meets a little S and M."

He burst out laughing. "I've never heard that before!"

"When I first started working for you I thought you were gay."

"Contrary to popular thought, not all Frenchmen are gay." He grabbed her hand. "And you know now that's not true."

Her breath caught at the electricity that shot between his hand to hers, like she had stuck her finger in a light socket. For a minute her toes curled. She looked down, away, and all around, anywhere but at him.

"You know, we must have eaten out a hundred times before," he mused and his thumb started to rub the skin on the back of her hand, "and you've never before asked me about my wardrobe."

"Was it a major faux pas?" She wanted to yank her hand away, yet at the same time no force on earth could make her move.

"I like it," he answered back. "You've worked with me for a year and we only know the superficial things about each other."

"That's not true," she protested, knowing she lied. She hadn't even known his taste in music and film until forced to ask. She eased her hand away from his. "All right, maybe so. But it's not like we've ever had to spend time together outside work."

"Wasn't for lack of not wanting, believe me," he murmured with a slight inflection in his tone that caused her to swallow and clear her throat. She looked into his eyes, and was nearly knocked off her chair. His eyes had grown darker, fierce, and focused entirely on her. They slowly wandered to her lips, leaving no doubt to exactly what he wanted now.

Her mind went blank, though thankfully she was saved from a comeback as the waitress arrived with their food, giving Penny a reprieve of sorts from the burn between her thighs. Shame on her for wanting to throw him down to the floor and have her wicked way with him. She thanked whatever deity had been listening that he wasn't wearing those damn black leather pants.

She grabbed her iced green tea and nearly downed it in one gulp before bringing the cool glass to up to her heated forehead, letting the condensation roll over her skin. She took a deep breath, put down her nearly empty glass, and proceeded to prepare her food.

Kiley looked at her funny. She just knew it. She didn't have to look back into those eyes of his to know an elegant eyebrow arched in her direction.

Sushi was an acquired taste. When she had first come out to Los Angeles from the back hills of Missouri, the idea of eating raw fish had been revolting. Watching people take bite after bite had turned her stomach, yet at the same time it was a fascinating world of the exotic, so Los Angeles. The quintessential "Let's do sushi" had replaced the catch phrase, "Let's do lunch." Kiley served it at all their shows with words like masago, ebi, and unegi, nothing American there. Completely posh.

Why would anyone even want to try it was the mental question she had every time she had came across it. Gradually she had experimented with cooked sushi. She'd had no choice, Kiley lived off the stuff—tempura, California Roll, vegetable roll. She had built up to eating miso soup and seaweed salad.

One night, after a particularly long grueling day of balancing out-of-town business clientele flying in for an upcoming show, where she hadn't had the opportunity to eat lunch, a whole tray of sushi had been delivered to Kiley and the guests he had downstairs. Starvation had been the key to everything. She had gone downstairs to find delightful looking rows of bright sushi and had stuffed as much food in her mouth as she could, not caring if it was raw or cooked.

Thank goodness it had been good sushi, from the very best restaurant around. Had it been horrible, her love of sushi would have died before it had begun. Fortunately, her queasy hesitation over it had ended and she had been born a new woman with excited taste buds.

She mixed her wasabi into the soy sauce and dunked a piece of tuna roll into it, the wasabi hot but not to the tongue. Instead the heat shot straight up into her nose and brought tears to her eyes. "Wonderful." She sniffed.

Kiley grinned. "You asked me a question, now I have one for you."

"All right." How bad could a question from him be? She took her glass of water glass and took a sip.

He leaned in slightly. "What do you know of S and M?"

She gasped and the water went down the wrong pipe. She started to cough. Kiley took the glass of water out of her hand so she wouldn't spill it. A full minute passed before her coughing subsided.

"You are so bad," she muttered, vowing never to take another drink in front of him again.

He chuckled. "And you are so easy. I suspect a girl from Missouri wouldn't have a clue to some of the fetishes the big city offers."

Her eyes narrowed. "For your information, most fetishes are born in small country towns because there's nothing else to do there. The businesses close at five sharp and nothing is open on Sundays except church and the Piggly Wiggly. In fact I read in the paper recently the Feds just busted a major meth lab twenty miles from my home town."

He pursed his lips and nodded as if impressed. "Am I going to find out you're a party girl?"

She snorted. "You forget, my favorite album is Enya and I have three teddy bears on my bed."

He went silent for a moment. His eyes glittered. "No, I didn't know that. But I bet you look adorable sound asleep, surrounded by your bears."

Her mouth went dry and the curious squirming sensation deep in her belly came back. She tried her best to ignore the quickening of her pulse. "Sentiments from my mom. I'm almost thirty and still can't sleep without something in my arms...I mean, they act as another pillow. I like to sleep on my stomach and they...oh, never mind."

"Penny," he said calmly. She hated how at ease he seemed when she went stumbling over every word.

"Yes?" she said testily.

He hesitated for a moment. "You know, I don't know if that is short for anything." It was an obvious attempt to lighten the tension that had suddenly developed and she jumped at it. Thank goodness he wasn't a stupid man.

"It's not. I still wish that my mom had named me something a little more sophisticated like Penelope or Persephone. Penny is such a little girl's name." She shrugged. "But what can you do? What about the name Kiley? That's not French."

"My parents had just moved back to Paris from New York when she discovered she was pregnant, and since my conception had been here, she wanted to give me something unique, something American."

"I like it. It fits you."

He raised an eyebrow. "Not too gay?"

She only laughed. The rest of the meal was quite pleasant, with small talk of various topics, but surprisingly not of art. For the first time, they dined as a man and a woman, not as a boss and his employee.

Somewhere, in the back of her mind, the memory of last night burned. Instead of treading water and biting her nails over "How could I?" and "What the hell?" she came the realization that, far from being uncomfortable with Kiley now, nothing really seemed different. In fact, he acted more consciously than before.

Could this be the ramification? If so, she wasn't too worried. What if he wanted more of what happened? More than just-this-one-night-only sex? She bit her lip and had to admit, the perks to their moment of sheer madness might not be too hard to bear.

After an hour and a half, he gestured for the check. Without looking at it, he handed his credit card over to the waitress.

"Do you talk with your parents often?"

He nodded. "About once a week. It gives me a chance to practice my French."

"I can't even tell you have an accent. Maybe in one or two words there's a distinction, a drawl, but I would never guess English wasn't your native language."

"I had a difficult time. For the French, harsh Germanic sounds are hard to pronounce. The French language tends to roll things out and flow together." The receipt came and he tallied up the tip and signed his name.

"I took Spanish as another credit in high school, but after three years dropped out. I had a big enough problem trying to figure out how to structure English sentences without throwing a foreign language in my brain."

He nodded along with her. "When I got to New York I knew only enough English to order pizza take out. I thought I'd never get the hang of the lingo. Consequentially, I can't stand eating pizza now." He rose and held out his hand to her. "Ready?"

Penny looked at the hand and ran her gaze up his arm to his eyes. They were warm, inviting, and she had the oddest feeling the hand being held out was offering her more than its innocent gesture.

Like a moth to a flame, she took it.

Who was she trying to kid? She wanted there to be a double innuendo behind his looks and words and actions. She had tasted his nectar once and she wanted more.

He held her hand as they maneuvered through the set tables and eating patrons. He waved good-bye with his free hand and led her out of the restaurant. Even outside he didn't drop her hand and she didn't pull away.

While they walked to his car, she thought that tonight had been odd. They had shared many meals together yet never once had any those dinners come to the intimacy that had occurred this evening. Their communication and lack of business talk had made the evening feel...like a date.

Did she and Kiley just have a date? He still held her hand, and they were strolling together, albeit in a parking lot, under the full moon. She wished she had seen which credit card he used, the company's or his personal one. She made a mental note to talk to Lark about this.

He held open his car door for her and she slid in. As she watched him walk around to the driver side she couldn't help but smile. Well, reflection or not, she had a week with him to figure out what the hell this all meant.

Chapter 6

His condo was one of those sultry high-rises with an amazing view over the ocean. Located on the harbor in Marina Del Rey, it was equipped with all the amenities of the price tag it carried. He turned his BMW into the underground parking where he had his own space, complete with his name painted on the pristine polished concrete. Together they took the private elevator right to his door.

"I'll get you a set of keys tomorrow," he told her as he led her through the foyer and into the den.

"I'm sure that's not necessary."

Kiley shook his head. "You should have one anyway, just in case something should happen to me."

She screwed up her face. "That's morbid."

He shrugged. "We're all going to go sometime, the question is when," he said philosophically.

She shook her head, mortality the last thing she wanted to hear about.

He flipped his car keys on a hall table and flipped on the lights before he turned to her. "Welcome to home, at least for the next week."

Their eyes met and the moment shifted. The world momentarily faded away. She completely forgot everything as the word "home" echoed in her brain and she licked her lips.

His eyes darkened a fraction before his head bent. She waited, breath held, anticipation tingling over every nerve. Lower and closer, she felt his breath on her lips.

Abruptly he pulled back, and the fire that he ignited cooled with a frigid blast of reality. He cleared his throat and turned away, running a hand through his hair.

"Right," he said hollowly. He took a deep breath and waved around carelessly with one hand. "This is the den, up there the bar and my desk. The business entertaining room, if you wish. To the hall down the right is the kitchen, dining room and the fun room. You'll find the TV and various other technology-oriented amusements. To the left," his finger zipped back, "are the bedrooms."

The quick, bland tour of his home gave her brain a much-needed breather from his overwhelming person. Kiley was sex on legs, and unfortunately she now knew how delicious sex was with him. Knew it, and wanted more.

His home was bright and bold, decorated in the same flair he gave all his life. The foyer had been white marble with half moon light fixtures, ala fifties style. The den walls were pale pink, a color barely there, and trimmed with a rough wooden timber motif. The paintings ranged from classical lines to modern chic and blended tastefully. The shag rug had various browns and pulled everything together.

A few sculptures sat back in the corners, women in various poses, a nod to the female form. Five steps from the den brought you up to another level, separated by a rail. A prominent glass-topped table dominated the room with papers strewn about. An art-deco cabinet stood directly behind it with various office machines, like a fax, printer, and copier. Left of that, on the same level, sported a bar, complete with a nicely stocked wine rack.

"I'll show you your room," he muttered and started down the left hallway.

Penny followed. He led her to a large, airy room in bright yellow. "My favorite color," she noted as she placed her bag on the bed.

He gestured to a door. "This is your bathroom."

She walked over and peeked in. "Wait," she said. "You said I had my own shower."

"Did I?" He shrugged apologetically. "I meant it had its own toilet."

"But where can I shower?"

"You'll have to use mine."

"There's not another shower?"

"There is a full guest bathroom down the other hall...."

"Great!"

"But I'm repainting."

Had that been a twinkle in his eye? She swore she saw one. "Fine, no problem, what could it hurt to share a shower with you?" It never failed, open mouth and insert foot, always at the time when she didn't need that to happen. "Er, that wasn't exactly what I meant."

He grinned and turned to head out of her room. She closed her eyes in embarrassment.

"Penny," he said. She opened her eyes and looked at him questioningly. "Anytime you want to share the shower, it's fine with me."

He walked out, shutting the door behind him. Great, just what she needed. Visions. Scenes poured into her head, of a waterfall, slick surfaces, the two of them plastered together as they shared soap. Suds sluicing over his chest, down his thighs. His hands roaming over her body, working the lather up. Where the water cleaned them away his mouth working magic. Up and down her neck, nibbles, sucking, bringing heat to life.

Penny moaned and fell across the bed, panting slightly. Sexual fantasies should be outlawed, especially when they involved the boss. Salacious thoughts poured through her mind as if a projector played. She couldn't keep her thoughts at bay.

Wetness flooded her panties, and with a trembling hand she pushed it down her jeans, pushing her panties aside. Her fingers met a slick mass as they brushed over her clitoris. A shiver streaked over her skin and down her back. Her left hand embraced her right breast, kneading it and tweaking her puckered nipple. A soft moan bled from her mouth and she bit her lower lip in an effort to be silent.

As she rubbed her clit with one finger, her other fingers dipped inside, brushing in sweeps as her lips swelled with lust. They rubbed together, causing a delicious friction as they rubbed against each other.

In her mind she saw Kiley from last night, poised above her as he rubbed against core. Instead of her hand rubbing her breast, she felt Kiley's hot breath as he took her nipple in his mouth and sucked, the heat of his mouth making her back arch off the bed. The fingers in her pussy became his swollen cock, plunging in without pause, speeding up as heat flushed over her skin.

Her palm ground down upon her cunt as her fingers pumped further. She felt the slick walls of her vagina sucking on them, as they must have sucked on him yesterday.

More, more, her breath rasped through her chest as a mist damped her skin. Juice ran down her thigh as the material of her jeans soaked it up. She was so close, so very close…

Faster and faster she rubbed her clit as the vivid image of Kiley above her and the memory of his whispered words slashed through her memory. Her pussy began to tighten as she spiraled out of control, her hips bucking wildly. She came hard, her fingers pumping through the waves of ecstasy. There was no stopping the moan that seeped from her mouth.

Afterwards, she lay there panting, hoping like hell he hadn't heard. Her heart thundered in response to her masturbation and lethargy started to settle in her bones. She took her hand out from her jeans and brought her wet fingers up to her lips, caressing them with her cum, wishing it Kiley's musk she tasted.

Penny spent the rest of the evening settling in, washing up in her small bathroom and changing her panties. At about eight she went to look for him, walking past the bathroom taped up and under construction. She found Kiley in the "fun room," as he had dubbed it, watching a movie. From the way his hair stuck up in the front she hazarded a guess he watched in deep concentration.

"Kiley?"

"Mm?" he mumbled.

"I'm going to take my shower now. I usually take one in the evening instead of the morning."

He picked up the remote to the TIVO and paused it.

"What are you watching?" she asked.

"A documentary on the possible use of lens distortion the Italian Renaissance painters might have used. Want to watch it with me? I can start over."

She bit her lip. She had read about the possibility from a magazine several months ago and had found the article fascinating, if not for the mere thought that if proven, it would shatter some concepts the art world viewed certain masterpieces.

"You don't mind?" she asked.

"Of course not." He picked up the remote, scooted over on the couch, and patted the warm space he had just deserted.

For the next two hours they watched and when certain interesting things caught their eyes, they would pause and talk about it. It was one of the most entertaining evenings Penny could remember in a long while, and not only from the fact that they were talking about the one thing each loved entirely. An ease existed between them, a comradeship she had never felt with any boyfriend from her past. Kiley talked to her on his level, as his equal, and it brought her a little more under his spell.

Finally, after the show ended, they sat in the muted den light. Kiley used the various remotes to flip off the TIVO machine and the high definition television.

"You know, I read a magazine article about this, and I hate to say it, but the arguments are very convincing," she murmured.

"I agree. I've seen many of the ones they focused on, like The Arnolfini Portrait, and remembering thinking along the same lines."

She bit her lip. "It's late, so if you don't mind, I'll take my shower tomorrow morning, after you of course."

"That's fine. I get up early so...anytime."

She wanted to stay and sit there with him, loathing to leave the groove they had found, but as a bell struck eleven somewhere in the condo, a yawn hit her. She stood and stretched and turned toward the doorway. "Good night, Kiley."

"Penny," he said her quietly and waited till she paused, her head turned sideways to see him. "I want you to be comfortable in my home."

They stood looking at each other in the soft light. She wondered what he would say if she told him she wanted to share his bed, and also wondered if she even had the guts. The debate raged inside her, the week she had with him...should she pursue it? But when the week ended, what would happen to them?

Her work had become the most important thing in her life, and Kiley fit into that musing. Perhaps Stu had been right. Her feelings for Kiley went deeper than being merely his assistant. Every decision she had made in the past year had been with him in mind. Could she give that up if the week went bad?

Did their one night together now make it a moot point?

She wished she knew the protocols of sleeping with the boss. Maybe she should read that book Lark bought for her. Should they ignore what happened and continue on? So far, except for the few times when he had tried to talk things out, everything seemed to fall back into place Kiley was still Kiley, and she...well, a tiny little part of her thought she was fast on her way to falling hard for her boss.

"Penny?" he asked quietly.

She snapped back to attention. "Yes?"

"Pleasant dreams."

"You too," she murmured and slipped around the corner.

Chapter 7

The morning came way too soon. She definitely was not a morning person, at least not before she had her very strong cup of espresso to shake the sleep from her eyes. She rolled over, squinted at the unfamiliar yellow bedroom, and remembered she would have to buy her daily dose of caffeine for the next week.

The dream she had been having, before the annoying buzz of her alarm had woken her, came blazing back in full force. It had been that damn waterfall fantasy she had been trying to avoid all last night through that documentary, when Kiley's leg had been pressed against hers. It somehow had morphed and twisted into a desert oasis love scene, complete with a French-talking Kiley riding up like Lawrence of Arabia to sweep her up onto his magic carpet of lust.

She wiggled around in the bed and realized that some time during the night, or during that carnal dream, her panties had become very wet and sticky. *Damn, what a dream.* She was half annoyed she hadn't been awake for her mind to fully enjoy it, though obviously her body had.

She threw back the comforter and wrinkled her nose at the actual prospect of getting out of bed and ready for work. Unequivocal, morning was the absolute worst part of the day. She rose and collected her clothes for the shower, along with her morning grooming kit. She cracked open her door and heard some sound coming from the far hall, near the kitchen and sighed in relief. She would be able to shower and erase the smell of sex caused from her very vivid dreams that clung to her skin like a beacon.

She walked a few steps down and entered Kiley's room, which had the door standing wide open in invitation. Of course, a few steps in and she had to pause to take in the very essence of Kiley. Bedrooms told a lot about a person, more so than the rest of the house, because it became the private domain of someone...their soul really. They could be perfect, orderly neat freaks in the rest of the house, and yet the bedroom would reflect their inner selves.

Dark blue with shards of red poking through in different areas such as his sheets, his comforter, and the finely woven carpet. His furniture matched, a modern design of black on black, which added to the dark yet enigmatic ambiance.

The unmade bed had pillows bunched up like he had been tossing and turning most of the night. Though there weren't any clothes of the floor, his open walk-in-closet showed signs of indecision. An exercise machine took up one corner and Penny assumed the torture device had something to do with the unbelievably tight abs and precision pecs he had.

Although all kinds of personal items littered about, she didn't play the snoop, though she wanted to. Instead, she took her time walking past everything into a very bright and steamy bathroom. Kiley had been and gone. Good, she'd have the place to herself and wouldn't have to worry about hurrying for his sake.

White tile decorated floor to ceiling with a long counter housing double sinks holding more hair, face and mouth products than she'd ever seen in her life. She thought she might dare try a few, wondering how different hair gel valued at $45 a bottle differed from Suave.

The sinks and shower were separate from the toilet area, which had its own door. An idea she thought to be well-designed. Never know when you had to keep the loo door closed for obvious reasons.

The shower was amazing. Large enough for probably four people, it had four different shower heads that spurted hot water in various, strategic points on the body, and even came with a bench that added to her waterfall fantasy.

She had a strong suspicion this would be filtering into her next wet dream, no pun intended. She lathered herself up, using her favorite rose scented glycerin soap. It wasn't terribly original, the scent, but she loved it. She washed her hair, rinsed off thoroughly, and spent at least ten minutes posing in front of each nozzle head to feel the full effect of the spray sting. When she turned off the water she stood for a moment, in the steam lined cubicle, squeezing out the excess water from her hair and enjoying the space that allowed her to do it.

Her own apartment was small, as most cheap apartments in Los Angeles tended to be, and she was lucky she had a small kitchenette, let alone a place to shower. She looked at some that consisted of one large room with the community bathroom down the hall. No way. She had splurged the extra two hundred per month for private facilities.

She slid open the glass door and grabbed the towel Kiley had thoughtfully left out for her, patting her body dry before running over her hair to get out as much moisture as possible.

A small noise interrupted her and she glanced absently at the doorway, taking in two things at once. First, she had left the door open. Second, Kiley stood there, watching her with a particularly dark gaze in his azure eyes. The look turned her knees to jelly and froze her like a deer in the headlights.

A thousand things swept across her mind, yet nothing stuck. She couldn't even remember if she was still breathing. One minute Kiley had been in the doorway with a mug of coffee, the next it shattered all over the white tile floor as he advanced on her.

He picked her up, the towel falling away, and sat her bare bottom on the counter ledge near the sink. The mirror had fogged over from the hot shower she had just finished. She randomly thought that a good thing so as not to see the wanton way she now seemed to be with her boss.

All thought disappeared. Their breaths mingled as their mouths met, tasting, twisting. He cupped her breasts, his thumbs rubbing along her nipples before slipping lower to tease her thighs open. Both thumbs rubbed her cunt, pressing into her slit with circular movements.

He wasn't gentle, but at that moment she didn't want him to be. She needed him to be quick, urgent and rough. She urged him on, mewling sounds of pleasure, skimming her own fingers over his chest and down that delicious ass of his. Black leather pants...again he had them on and she pulled impatiently at the soft material.

He must have understood her unspoken need because he moved slightly away, bringing his hand to the front of his zipper. The material shifted and he pressed into her, filling her, fucking her in deep thrusts.

"Yes," she muttered, lost. She flung her head back as he rode her, hard, on the counter between his shaving cream can and her toothbrush. A hand went behind her, against the mirror, steadying them as she raised her legs to wrap around him.

He grunted in her ears and bit softly on her lobe. "God, you feel good," he rumbled into the soft skin right below. "Yes...squeeze me...*Mon Dieu....*"

He returned one thumb to where they joined, hitting the soft nub of her and stimulating it with every thrust. She moaned and thrust out her chest just as she exploded in a gazillion pieces.

"I'm going to come," he hissed in pleasure. "I'm going to fucking come..."

He grabbed her hips, holding them as he moaned deep in his throat, almost guttural and stiffened.

Their spasms rocked together and he collapsed against her, his sweaty forehead dropping onto her shoulder and her own head leaning against the mirror.

"I couldn't sleep last night," he finally said in a low, melodic voice, "knowing you lay in the next room." He raised his head and looked at her with deeply glowing eyes. His gaze dropped to her lips, following an instant later as his head dipped and his mouth fitted to hers.

As kisses went, it would have knocked her socks off had she been wearing any. It started as a nibble but grew into a passionate heating of their bloods. His hands came up and started caressing her breasts, and though he should have been worn out from their mind-shattering mutual climax, she felt him growing inside her.

It was a sensation she had read about, but had never felt, and she decided it was the most erotic feeling she had ever had. It gave her a sense of power that this man, this Greek Adonis, withered under her touch. Before long they rocked back and forth again, moaning.

Needless to say, they were late for work.

They showered again, together yet separately in the cubicle, and dressed in separate bedrooms. Kiley had cleaned up the shattered mug and spilt coffee while she sat on her own bed wondering how this could happen, twice, in almost as many days.

They were quiet as they rode the elevator down to the parking level, and for that Penny was grateful. Her thoughts spun, even as her satiated body rejoiced. She was fast coming to love those black leather pants of his.

They didn't say a word to each other during the ride, though it wasn't an uncomfortable ride to the gallery. Penny sensed Kiley thought about what had happened, same as her, and needed some quiet time to reflect that their relationship had taken a deeper, albeit twisted, turn.

When she finally sat down at her desk, an hour later than usual, she found several messages waiting for her attention, as well as a notice that the Fed-Ex driver would be back around noon. Kiley disappeared into the kitchen to make coffee.

The day started and with such an interesting beginning, and she wondered how the night would progress.

Chapter 8

It was close to five when Lark called.

Kiley had gone down into the gallery to manage things again. Privately, Penny thought it an excuse to keep busy because they had had a quiet day, but she didn't say anything. She figured he had as much a difficult time coming to terms banging his assistant as she had about banging the boss.

"Papillon's," she answered in a pleasant, monotone voice.

"Did you read the book? Any good advice?" Lark said by way of greeting.

Penny immediately lost all semblance of control. "Read it? I think I bloody well could tell that author a thing or two."

"What happened?" From her tone, Lark had guessed what had happened, but like any good voyeur she wanted details.

"This morning, that's what happened," Penny moaned and shot a quick glance at the door, making sure the entrance empty. Then she went into every lurid detail, including him slipping in that sexy little French phrase. "We had an amazing dinner and he held my hand. Does that mean something? Later we watched a movie. When I finally went to sleep I had this amazing dream…whoa…when I woke up my panties were drenched... Okay, too much information there, but after I had taken my shower he walked in, and…Lark, are you there?"

She had been rambling, and rambling quite quickly, but once the dam broke she couldn't seem to hold any of her thoughts back. She heard a stunned, "Uh huh," from Lark and that launched her into a whole different track.

"So what do I do? What would you do? I'm living with him for a week, my room is right next to his. If I wanted, I could put my ear to his door and hear him snoring, if he snores. And I still have to face that shower every morning, whether he's in it or not, but I'm hoping he is. Hell, I'm hoping he wants me back in his bed tonight. Is that wrong? He's my boss for cripes sake. Lark, tell me what to do."

Her voice ended on a high pitched whiney note, not very attractive and definitely too damsel in distress. Penny sighed and leaned back in her chair.

"Sorry," she said into the mouthpiece.

"Do you feel better?"

"Much," she said. "Thanks, I just had to get that out of my system."

"For what it's worth, I think you should stop thinking so hard on the long term consequences and the road not taken. It's all bullshit anyway," Lark said, and Penny could swear she heard a bit of giggle in her tone. "Live in the now, girlfriend. Live in the now."

"Are you laughing at me?"

She paused and gave a discreet cough. "Never, sweetie. Would I do that? Don't answer that. As for that book, I'll keep my eye out. Maybe, "Fall of the Divine Secretary Slash Assistant." Listen, I gotta run. The director of this episode is screaming so I gotta peddle some pushers. Love ya."

She hung up and the line went dead. Penny stared at the receiver for a full minute, feeling slightly betrayed by Lark's cheerful tone while she, Penny, felt anything but.

"Something wrong?" Kiley asked from the doorway.

She started and slowly hung up. "No, just Lark."

He raised a finely shaped brow.

"Confirming Sunday. We have a date Sunday," she replied.

He leaned against the doorframe. "For the ready-to-talk mode?"

Penny's mouth dropped a fraction. How had he known? "Um" was as far as her eloquence would go.

Kiley pushed from his lean and moved to sit in the chair in front of her desk. "Will you talk with me?"

Uh oh. The talk. Was she ready for this? Did she have a choice?

She nodded and thought she saw him let out a relieved breath. He folded his hands together across his stomach. He looked calm and collected.

"This morning was...."

Unexpected? A mistake? Circumstantial? Pretty fucking good?

"...Pretty fucking good," he finished.

She blinked. Did she think that out loud? Obviously not, since he continued talking.

"I've spent all day thinking about the other night, and now this morning, about the reasons why it's a bad idea for this to have happened. I'm your boss. You're my employee. Yada yada yada." He raked a hand through his elegantly styled hair. "But I want you to know that I won't let this interfere with our working relationship."

That was exactly what she wanted hear. Wasn't it? If so, why did she suddenly feel so hollow inside?

"Penny?" he prompted.

She smiled widely, and if it seemed a bit too over bright, he didn't comment. "Wonderful. I'm so glad you think that way. I've been thinking things over and I figured out it had to be the pants."

He blinked. Clearly he wasn't tying to two incidences together. "The pants?"

She flicked a finger at him. "Those black leather pants." She shook her head. "When I see them on you, I just want to molest you right out of them. And God help me for the honesty bug that's bitten me."

He didn't react for a moment, he only stared at her in a manner that released about a thousand butterflies in her stomach. She wished she had super powers in that moment. She'd love to read what flashed though his mind.

The smile he unleashed affected the butterflies in a completely different way. "Put the phone on the machine."

"Why?"

"We're going out."

"All right," she replied curiously. "For the show?"

He shook his head as he watched her closing up her desk, turning on the answering service and shutting down her computer. "For a date."

She almost fell out of her seat. "Ex...excuse me?"

He stood and held out his hand to her. She looked at it first before glancing into his eyes. He winked and that flirtation that made her take his hand and let him lead her to his car.

Los Angeles was a terrific place to experience anything. You could do the more serious side of learning or just take things easy and sample all life had to offer in a melting pot of distinct flavors and titillation. You had the heavy ethnic flare or you had the more traditional route of American culture. That night, he offered her the later, a night of fun and simple enjoyment.

He took her to Universal City Walk, which figured around six to eight city blocks, and boasted shops, eateries, restaurants, a huge movie complex, and musical entertainment. He took her to a duo piano bar on the second landing. Two pianos sat facing each other, each with a piano player who complemented each other, taking turns singing and incorporating the audience. Penny had fun, watching the perfectly groomed and polished Kiley Laurent sing off-key along with piano men as they took requests and played musical hits from all over the timeline. The requests Kiley made varied and over several hours, and several mixed drinks, Penny completely lost her inhibition and joined with him.

Somewhere, in the four hours inside the piano bar, Kiley's hands had strayed to hers, and he never let go. If he got up to dance, she went with him. If he sat down, her hand rested in his lap. The only time he let go of her was when either of them had to go to the bathroom.

At one point, during a particularly slow song, when he had pulled her to the dance floor and they swayed back and forth, they looked at each other realizing exactly where the evening would wind up.

They left right after the song ended. Kiley waved at the piano players, gave them each a nice tip, and led her quickly out the door and into the garage where.

It was late, and hardly anyone was around as they climbed the stairs. In fact, his car was the only one in his section of the parking structure. When he walked up and clicked the unlock button from his key chain, he pushed her up against the passenger side, sliding in between her jean clad legs.

More than ready, one hand slid up his arm while another tangled in his head to pull his mouth to hers. She raised one leg to wrap the calf around his.

He moaned. "You're driving me crazy," he muttered in her ear, just before he bit the lobe. "I got nothing done today. I kept thinking about fucking you this morning."

His tongue traced down the side of her neck. She panted and stretched her hand down between them to grab him. "Do you have any idea how turned on I am?" she whispered to him.

"God, I want you. Here, now." He claimed her lips and the thrust of his tongue mimicked the thrust of his hips.

And right there, in full of view of anyone who should happen by, with security cameras probably catching every moment on tape, Kiley touched down with his own hand and unbuttoned and unzipped her jeans. He pushed his hand in until his fingers skimmed her pussy lips, which elicited a low moan from her.

One finger massaged her while another slipped in, hitting the nub that made her breath catch in her throat and forget their surroundings. He knew exactly how to work her, using deep, slow strokes, igniting the fire until the moment she needed it faster and harder.

As she neared climax he bent over and captured her sound with his mouth, kissing the sensation from her and using that to share her pleasure. Her hands traveled down from his shoulders to open the fly of his pants.

"I want you inside me," she whispered, a naughty glint shining in her eyes. Her tongue came out to lick her bottom lip.

"Here?" he whispered back, though he didn't even look around. As she worked his pants, he worked on jeans and panties. He gave a gasp as her hand closed over his cock, bringing it free from its confine to massage it up and down the shaft.

When her jeans low enough, Kiley grabbed one leg and brought it up while bending his knees. The slightly awkward angle brought the glistening tip even with her slick opening.

"Here? With potential eyes watching our every move?" he murmured into her ear. He swiveled his hips, and instead of pushing in, the hard cock head bumped into her clit.

"Fuck me, Kiley," she panted, arching her pelvis.

In one hot thrust, he sheathed himself tight, eliciting a groan from both. He held still for a moment, resting his forehead against hers as if savoring the moment.

"Fuck, you're tight," he grated as he brought his hips back, bringing his cock to the tip of her opening, only to slide back in with an abrupt thrust.

Kiley's hands grasped her ass, getting a firm grip as he started to increase the pressure of his deep penetration. She tunneled her face into his neck, found the pulse that beat under his skin, and bit gently. With that slight pressure of pain, all semblance of gentleness vanished as he started bucking against her needful pussy.

She let out a wail of pleasure as he started to hammer her, angling her pelvis to get him deeper. Over and over he slammed her, both concentrating on the feel of being animalistic in such a public place, knowing at any moment they could be caught.

With a howl Kiley started to erupt. With each blast of cum he thrust once, twice, and the third hit the bundle of nerves inside her, setting off her own climax. She clamped down on him, seeing stars as they floated down from the plateau they had fallen off of.

Her leg fell from his hip and his hands released their grip. It took a few minutes for their breathing to slow down.

"Holy hell," he muttered, his forehead resting against hers once again.

"I hope that doesn't end up on YouTube." She giggled.

He raised his head and looked down at her, smiling. They pulled apart slowly and adjusted their clothing, Penny extremely aware of the juices coating her thighs.

He opened the door to his BMW for her and she slid onto the leather, her head falling back in relaxed satiation. As soon as that sexy rear of his touched down into the driver's side, the phone attached to his dashboard rang. Both stared at it like it strange anomaly, temporarily clueless on why it should be ringing at that particular moment.

Kiley squinted and bent his head a little lower, and groaned. As soon as he hit the talk button, Jedidiah Yuki's voice came booming over the speaker.

"I've been ringing you all night!" the artist whined. "I'm in a terrible frame, just terrible, Kiley!"

Kiley sighed. He had once told her that he hated the way Jedidiah said his name, dragging out the last syllable and having the 'ley' sound like 'leeeee'. "What's wrong, Jed?" he replied and Penny had to admire the way his tone came out soothing and gentle.

"I've been thinking about the 'Blue Anger' line for the show and I don't think people are going to get the message. We need darker, bolder, we need Slasher. Picture this: gunmetal gray, maroon, black noir. Axes, knives...."

"Guns?" Kiley broke in and he snatched the phone off its cradle, the same time as he started the engine.

What a way to kill the moment, Penny thought. But in a way, glad the pause had come. It gave her a breather she suspected she needed. She leaned back and turned her head to stare out the passenger window as Kiley drove them home, half listening to the one-sided conversation, "No, you do that, Jed, and I will punch you in the face. No, I can't push the fucking show date back." While her mind played through the events of the day, it skipped over the morning and work schedule to fly right into the "date."

She was getting in too deep, too deep and too quickly. The emotions churning inside her were nothing she'd ever felt before, but she no longer worried about the taboos listed for a boss and assistant. Instead, what bothered her now was the very real love creeping up on her.

As she watched the lights of her new home come closer she pushed aside the little voice that warned her of trying to simplify the complicated situation to her heart.

Kiley continued to still on the phone with Jed after they had walked in the front door. He walked straight through his foyer to his glass-topped desk to flop into his comfy-looking leather swivel seat. Penny locked up behind him and placed his keys on the table he had dumped them on last night. She noticed a matching set and realized they must be for her.

She left them there.

She stood for a second in the dim light, watching him. He ran a hand though the front of his hair, tangling it, a frustrated gesture she knew very well.

"Jed, come to Papillon's tomorrow and we can go over your inventory."

Penny smiled and turned, heading down the hallway...to her bedroom.

"Jed, wait...wait!" He held the phone to one side. "Penny!"

She turned.

He gestured impotently at the phone. "I'll get off as soon as possible."

She smiled at him. "You've got work." She raised a hand. "I'll see you tomorrow."

She blew him a kiss and headed to her own bedroom.

Chapter 9

Jedidiah beat them there.

A short man with dark Asian features of his surname and short spiky hair, Penny liked him even though when he showed up an emotional mess followed. He needed a strong hand to guide him. Like all proficient artists, and the dead ones he tried to emulate, his mind never stopped working, and he often forgot that other people didn't have the same insomniac drive he did. Which was one reason he had no problem calling Kiley at odd hours of the morning, day, and evening, or showing up to wait at Papillon's two hours before it opened. He was eccentric, erratic, and utterly charming.

"Where have you two been?" he asked as soon as they stepped out of Kiley's BMW. "Hello, Penny, love, grand morning. You look totally smashing, as usual. Kiley, have you thought over my Slasher theme?"

Penny thought she heard Kiley's back teeth grind together. Poor man. She had woken up after a restless night sleep in her yellow room, made sure Kiley wasn't anywhere near his bedroom, and ran and locked the bathroom door. For all her flip analysis of their situation, she had decided somewhere between four-fifteen and six-thirty am, that there are some lines one shouldn't cross, such as giving candy to babies, taking money from victim relief jugs, and sleeping with the boss. No, not sleeping, just fucking.

For heaven's sake, she had just broken up with her boyfriend seventy-two hours ago. Did her behavior mirror something closer to a rebound, or did the breakup just release the inhibition of her mind?

She had always liked and respected Kiley, did she unknowingly love him all this time as well?

Lost in her own little world, Penny hadn't said anything to him the entire ride to work and, thankfully, he had seemed to sense her mood. Now, Jed Yuki stood there to monopolize all their time.

"Jed, I haven't had my second cup of coffee. Kiley sighed as he disarmed the gallery and held the door open for both.

"I can go out and buy us some cappuccinos," the artist volunteered, once again missing the pointed reference.

Kiley waved his hand. "I'll make it," he grumbled and practically ran up the stairs to disappear into the kitchen.

His abrupt departure allowed Jed to turn his brilliant idea onto her. "Did he tell you my vision, Penny?" He clasped his hands together as if he were a little boy getting ready to share some special revelation. "We have the section called 'White Hope' so why not a section that transplants into a one-eighty? Love and light meets the ultimate death in all its eviscerated digestion."

One side of Penny's lips contorted in a yuck gesture. "Isn't that what 'Blue Anger' shows?"

"Yes, but without the disembowelment. Without the bile rolling stomachs. Without the gripping reality of absolute death. Besides, it's so blue."

Penny thought that was the point, but held back refrain in case he went on another breakfast-turning bender.

Jed clapped in wild exuberance before spreading his hands out and painting the air with them both. She noticed both hands were drawing their own picture, separate of each other.

He caught her interested look. "I've got a photographic memory too," he told her.

"Excuse me?"

He lowered his hands from their independent compositions. "Both sides of my brain can work simultaneously apart from each other, which also lets me remember everything."

"I bet that can be annoying."

He chuckled. "You're the first person to nail it on the head. Which is one reason why 'Blue Anger' doesn't work." He put one hand on her shoulder. "It's all black inside here." With his other hand he pointed to his head. "I've lived with it too long. I have to get Slasher out."

There was something frightfully chilling in his matter-of-fact tone. Just the casual way he talked about something so dark and disturbing inside him that made Penny pull away. "Good luck trying to convince Kiley to change the format around."

Jed nodded tiredly. "I've been painting furiously. Once he sees my work he'll agree." Just like that, the dark mood passes and once again the jolly artist she knew emerged, leaving her to wonder if she had imagined the Edgar Allen Poe personality.

"Jed," Kiley called from the top of the stairs. "Get into the Green Room and wait for me, please. Let my secretary get to her desk."

"My my, snobbish much?" Jed said, not in the bit ashamed of voicing his thoughts out loud. "Weren't you talking to Penny last night while at your home?" He turned to face her, asking the same question he had just asked Kiley. "Wasn't he talking to you last night at his house?"

Her mouth opened and closed. Not a peep came out, so Jed turned back to looking up the stairs at Kiley.

"You did," Kiley replied calmly. "Her car is broken, it's getting fixed. Penny is staying in my guest bedroom. Not that it's any of your business, Jed. Now, would you please go into the Green Room and wait for me?"

Jed pursed his lips, turned back to Penny, and gave her a knowing smirk, before he headed to the Green Room where he had been told, twice, to wait. In the case of Papillon, the Green Room had been painted in swirls of red highlighted in deep yellow, to give energy.

Penny had supervised its painting and decorating and had been really proud of how it turned out. Ethan Allen meets Lay-Z-Boy. The two big love seats in the room were plush with lots of pillows and even the freestanding chairs had padded seats to help keep the old bum from going to sleep.

She had ventured one weekend to the Venice Boardwalk to peruse the local artists selling their wares and had come across a woman selling the most adoring tiny portraits of silhouettes against the fading backdrop of the setting sun. The colors shone vibrantly and Penny had bought all she had. They hung proudly on the wall in a nod to Los Angeles's bohemian culture. She got many compliments on them and had been proud to have caused the young woman's sales to increase. She made a point to visit the artist every once in a while to say hello.

She trudged up the stairs watching Kiley as he watched her. He held out a mug of coffee to her before turning toward the office. She followed, sipping her strong brew, glad to at least have another fortification of caffeine hitting her nervous system. Better to blame the butterflies on that than the effect Kiley had on her.

He dressed today in a pair of faded black jeans, though you could tell they had been worn by fashion and not from regular wear. He wore a white button down shirt with it, open at the collar and not tucked it. The ends helped hide his fantastic ass, a blessing and a curse. His hair slightly rumpled, each strand held in place with gel, in an adorable messy shag. It made a girl want to run her fingers through it to straighten it out.

On most men such meticulous care of their appearance would be considered ridiculous, even unmanly. When little girls are growing up they dream of rugged manly men, part cowboy and part business man, men who said they never cried, but who secretly would break down at the thought of losing the girl forever. At least, that had been the type of man Penny had dreamed of.

But with Kiley, his brand of magnetism drew her like a moth to a flame. With his European golden looks, strong patrician nose, high jutted cheekbones and firm yet full lips, he knew he looked good, but it was the cocky confidence that made him devastating to stare at. It *made* you want to stare.

He sat in front of her desk and waited while she made herself comfortable, resting one leg on the opposite knee.

"What's wrong?" he asked as soon as she turned to give him her full attention.

She blinked. "Beg pardon?"

His foot jangled. "You've been quiet all morning, and now you have this look on your face like you stepped in dog shit."

"Did you really have to call me your secretary in such a tone of voice? And I prefer assistant, rather than secretary."

The foot stopped bouncing. "I didn't mean anything by that. I was trying to get Mr. Happy Pants the hell away from you."

"Why? He wasn't hurting anyone."

"He's a nuisance."

"Since when?"

"Since eleven last night!" He sighed, the foot went down and he shifted to run a hand through this hair. So much for the hip style. "Listen, there is something between us we need to get out."

What was *that* supposed to mean? A slow burn started in her stomach. "Get out? Where do you want it to go?"

"Don't be dense, Penny."

The burn started to heat up. "Dense about what, Kiley? The fact that I've fucked my boss? Or the fact I might have misconstrued it all?"

"What the hell are you talking about?"

"I don't know, you're the one calling me dense!"

She had never realized her voice could go so high.

He stood and slammed his cup onto her desk. "Obviously dense is the correct word here. The context is stimulating, really, but I've got a client waiting below."

"By all means, don't let me keep you," she muttered sourly.

He gurgled a strangled sound deep in his throat and turned to storm out, pausing at the door to look at her. "We will talk about this later," he growled and stomped away.

Penny blinked back tears that had suddenly appeared, her anger leaving her as quickly as it had surfaced. Men could be really obtuse sometimes. She leaned her head in her hands while she sniffed and tried to reign in the explosive emotions that had burst to the surface.

Great, where had all that come from? She rarely ever got angry, and yet within moments she had been screaming at Kiley like a banshee. Had it been her sleepless night or something else? She wondered if she could figure it out properly if A) she could separate her emotions, B) get Kiley's kiss out of her brain, and C) get Kiley out of her emotions.

She was afraid it might be too late for that.

Luckily for her the day was busy. At nine the phone started ringing and it never ceased, which wasn't unusual since the show was next weekend. In fact, she pretty much counted her days being run ragged. Deliveries came, inspections came, and the day didn't offer any relief.

It was rare that she and Kiley argued. One of the reasons he hired her was because they hit it off with similar thoughts, similar construction on art criticism and the love of same artists. But it went deeper than that. During her interview she had completed several of his sentences, communicating in a way that two people who must have worked twenty years side by side did.

Now they had fought. Their first fight. Her first scream-like-a-banshee fight. Over something she had no idea what. There could be only one conclusion to make...

Sex had to be the reason.

In her hectic day, where Kiley avoided the office from either a lack of desire to see her or because since nine that morning he had been stuck between answering the phone and a pleading Jed, she calmed down enough to come up with a plan of action.

It hurt her to have this misunderstanding hanging between them. Kiley wasn't just her boss, but her best friend, and the man she happened to be falling in love with.

That revelation hit her in the middle of a conversation with the florist as they were double checking the order she had placed last month. He had said "white roses," and her brain dissolved, flashing to a wedding scene with her and Kiley standing on top of the wedding cake feeding each other icing.

She now realized the reason why she could never give Stu her undivided attention, even at the most intimate moments. The reason why it had been so easy to fall into Kiley's arms the night after her break-up. The reason why she became hot and bothered whenever he came into the room. The reason why her temperature raged whenever their skin touched. The reason why she became sick at the thought of ever watching him walk away.

Oh god. Ohgodohgodohgodohgodohgodohgod.

"Uh, Penny?" came the hesitant voice through the phone.

"Yes?" she croaked.

"Are you all right?"

Sheesh, what a question! She nodded and then realized the florist, Jaime, couldn't see her. "Yeah, fine. I just found out some disturbing news."

"Not about the show I hope?"

"No, not that. Jaime, everything sounds fine. At least what I heard of it, it did. Can I call you tomorrow to go over it again?"

"Sure thing, Penny," Jaime assured. "Hope you're feeling better."

He hung up and so did she, reaching over slowly and flicking on the answering service. The clock said three in the afternoon. She hadn't had a bathroom break all day, her stomach growled and she just discovered she was in love with Kiley.

Someone shoot her now.

As she walked into the tiny kitchen to get some food from the delivery earlier (Chinese she noted), she thought at least the day couldn't get much worse. And it was Thursday. Tomorrow was Friday, sure to be busy. Sunday she planned on a date with Lark so that left only one day free with Kiley.

She sat at the table and ate her heated up vegetable fried rice, washing it down with an orange soda. She usually tried to avoid soda altogether, but today she needed comfort, and her comfort food happened to be orange soda. She could drink it with anything, any time of the day, and thus tried to avoid the highly sugar-filled drink. Since she didn't really have time to exercise, she had to make allowances in her diet or else she would balloon up.

Penny finished her lunch and washed her hands, making a quick trip to the bathroom. As she turned the office corner, she mentally corrected her belief that the day couldn't get worse.

It did. Kiley's sister stood there, smiling gorgeously, waving to her, and next to her stood a drop-dead beautiful brunette. Kiley stood with one arm folded around his waist and the other running a hand through his hair. Jed used his fingers to frame the models for a painting.

"*Bonjour!*" Antoinette cried out, rushing up to throw her arms around Penny in a hug.

In all fairness, Antoinette was extremely nice. They had met twice before, when she was in town visiting Kiley, and each time they had gotten along famously. Antoinette proclaimed to be in love with Hollywood movie stars, so they had gushed over fashion and gossip magazines together, giggling like schoolgirls. She was a feminine version of her older brother and a model: blonde hair, big blue eyes, and a size zero. Honestly. Penny had never thought such a size existed until she went shopping with her once. Once. How depressing it turned out to be trying on clothes with a girl who couldn't even wear a number.

For a week afterward Penny had eaten nothing but vegetables, but all that accomplished was to make her go to the bathroom more.

Being a model meant Antoinette was able to visit Los Angeles several times a year. Mainly she operated out of France and New York, but on occasion took assignments on the West Coast to visit with Kiley.

And Penny adored her. Really. It was only the fact that Penny now occupied the bedroom that Antoinette usually stayed in when in town. Antoinette said something gleeful in French, to which Penny shook her head in a helpless gesture. Kiley said something back, in French, which caused his sister to wave dismissal.

"*Oui*, I know," she said and then translated, "I told Kiley I didn't mind sleeping on his couch."

"Oh, really, I can...."

"And this is my very close friend, Sharla." Antoinette sent her a conspiratorial wink. "I thought I'd bring her to let Kiley have a little fun while I'm working."

Yep. Goody gum drops.

Chapter 10

Later that night, Penny found herself wedged in between the mirrored wall and Antoinette while she watched Sharla apply flirtatious love pats over Kiley's arms, shoulders and, she could only imagine, places below the table.

She had somehow been coerced into dinner and pool, and tried to figure out the exact moment when she said yes instead of "I have to wash my hair." Truth be told, it wasn't hard to drift from the topic of conversation, considering she didn't understand the language that the other three dinner guests spoke.

They had ended up at a sports bar on the Third Street Promenade, one of the main attractions of Santa Monica. The small shopping street extended for three blocks, and held little boutiques of bookstores, clothing stores, shoe stores, theaters, eateries and odds-n-ends. Musicians and street performers plied their art for tips among the tourists. Grassy dinosaurs kept watch and sprouted water to form a fountain at each end. Bright lights kept everything lit in a warm atmosphere and lent a type of magical charm over everyone.

Inside the sports bar, televisions blared different games from basketball to football to soccer. Rock and roll poured from speakers making ordinary conversation difficult. The food was better than average for such a spot, though overpriced due to the locale. Penny ordered pasta with large shrimp, and watched in consternation as Miss Skinny 1 and Miss Skinny 2 nibbled on their salads.

Even though it was a Thursday night, the bar filled up fast. Kiley smiled at Sharla, removed her hand from his thigh, and walked up to the pool counter to obtain a table and balls.

"I asked Sharla and Toni if they had ever played American pool," Kiley said to her as he chalked his stick.

"Mm," Penny replied. She had stayed silent as Antoinette had paired them off, them partnered together while Sharla got cozy with Kiley. Penny had to fight down the urge to claw the model's eyes out.

Kiley broke the balls and managed to sink the five ball. He walked around the table eyeing his next target while Sharla teased him and asked him questions, practically rubbing her body up and down his like a feather duster. Really, all she needed was the little French maid outfit.

With his attention distracted, he missed his next shot. Antoinette stepped up. She knocked the cue ball in.

Kiley said something in French and immediately Sharla started wiggling her butt like a French poodle as he placed the cue ball at the end of the table. They spoke rapidly to each other as Kiley bent over her to help her hold her stick and line up a target.

Penny watched the interplay, hopping the pasta she ate wouldn't come back up. It was no surprise that the French airhead didn't hit a thing.

Penny smiled tightly at Kiley and Antoinette and studied the table. By this time, a burning had started in her stomach and she wanted to be anywhere other than right there watching the French doxy make cooing sounds at Kiley.

With absolute precision and skill, Penny went after her first ball. The ten, cornered. The nine, banked into the side. The twelve, shot straight with a crack. The eleven hit the fourteen and sank it. The eleven she barely touched to let it follow. The thirteen and fifteen easily dispatched into corners. All that remained was the eight. She eyed it, called it into a side, and cracked the cue into it. It rolled sharply right where she said, the cue left spinning in one place. She smiled, handed her stick to Antoinette, holding out her palm to Kiley.

"Can I take the car home? I've got a headache."

Secretly, she wallowed in the shock and jaw-hanging expressions on their faces. Kiley's blue eyes twinkled at her as he tossed her the keys.

"We gotta talk about those pool skills you forgot to mention," he murmured.

She couldn't keep the self-satisfied smirk off her face as she turned and left.

* * * *

Several hours later, Penny clicked off the giant high definition television after watching one of Kiley's DVDs. She stretched and then headed toward the kitchen area to grab a glass of milk before heading to bed.

Penny had been highly impressed with Kiley's powerful little car. She wondered how she could word it in order for her to borrow it, say up past the 101/405 juncture, where the traffic thinned out enough for her to take it up to ninety.

In any case, she had driven back to the condo and used her set of keys to get it. The place was hers. Mmmm, what sort of trouble could she get into?

Actually, she became very pragmatic. She took a quick shower, washed and dried her hair and even took the opportunity to put on a facemask, a la influence of Antoinette. She had packed all her stuff up and moved into the fun room. The couch would be comfortable enough for the night, and tomorrow she would beg Lark to pick her up so she could spend the weekend, thus giving Kiley and Antoinette needed bonding time.

The kitchen was reminiscent of a Spanish hacienda with russet and tan tiles and black wrought iron. An island allowed one to wash and prepare vegetables and had four bar stool-type chairs for easy eating. The dining room opened to the kitchen through an arch, but Kiley strung up a beaded gateway that added ambiance to the room.

But it wasn't the kitchen or the dining room that had caught her eye. Rather the magnificent balcony extending from the kitchen, over the Pacific Ocean, which took her breath away. Forgetting the milk, she walked to the glass doors and opened them.

The night breeze hit her like a warm blanket. It wrapped around her and pulled her to the railing. The dark ocean rumbled in the distance. The full moon overhead lent a thousand stars and illuminated the gentle swells of the water below as the tide moved in.

The balcony had potted trees and plants, a glass-topped table with cushioned chairs, and in the corner, under an awning, stood an easel. So, that's where he did his painting. She wondered if he had been painting for his own recreation, his own pleasure. A canvas rested on it, draped to allow the breeze in but keep any debris off. Though curiosity ate at her, Penny turned away, back to the ocean.

Her hands gripped the railing until her knuckles turned white. There was nothing more she wanted to do than peep at Kiley's work, especially work in progress, but it was a confidence issue. He never invited her to see it, and she felt like she couldn't impose.

Art to some became an expression of their soul, the journey of the painting either a revelation or a redemption. Penny had seen some of Kiley's work from his New York era days, and had loved the bold, abstract voice he painted in. But he said he put away being the artist in favor of being the bearer who brought other artist to life. A sacrifice he said was the right choice for his particular love of art.

Penny knew how to draw, paint, and create in the abstract sense, but she lacked the key element all successful artists had. And if one didn't know what that element was no amount of studying helped. Kiley had had it. He had been successful as an artist in New York and she agreed with the critics. It was one of the reasons why she had been thrilled to work with him when the opportunity had arisen.

Why she was desperate not to let anything happen to their affinity.

"Beautiful, isn't it?" Kiley's deep voice broke calmly through her musings.

She felt him standing there. Somehow, in her musings of him, he appeared. Yet she kept staring over the night. "I can't imagine living my life without the ocean. It's so peaceful, so calming."

"I feel the same way." He came to stand next to her. "The Atlantic around New York is cold, harsh. The best beaches are down south, near South Carolina or Georgia, and it's pretty there, but the first time I hit the Pacific Ocean I knew I had found home."

"Even over Paris?"

He nodded. "Much to the consternation of my mother."

Penny grinned. "Is she one of those mothers who's always harping for you to settle down and raise her some grandbabies?"

He laughed. "How did you know?"

"I hear it myself every weekend."

Antoinette came out to join them. "Penny, I would have slept on the couch."

She felt Kiley's eyes swing her way. "The sheets need to be changed. I didn't know where the extras were located."

Antoinette waved the remark off. "We shall take turns, *oui*? Share the bedroom!" She laughed like they shared a great joke.

"Actually, tomorrow I'm going to ask my friend Lark to let me stay the weekend with her. It shouldn't be a problem. They don't have production on the weekend."

Brother and sister spoke at once.

"*Non!*" Antoinette protested. "I am the unexpected guest."

"Penny, that's not—"

Penny held both hands up. "Kiley, I thank you so much for lending me your home, but things have changed."

Those last four words suddenly brought it out in vivid color. They both knew it. Kiley's eyes narrowed and Penny's went wide. Tension, thick and complicated, roared between them. Everything else faded away, including Antoinette's curious ears.

"That's not true," Kiley stated emphatically.

"It is, Kiley, and you know it."

He grabbed her upper arm. "You're pushing away because you can't deal."

"You're absolutely right, I can't deal. Too fast, too soon. If you stop and think about it, you know I'm right. Where do you think this can possibly end?"

"You're giving up," he accused, anger tightening the smooth skin around his mouth. "Before you even know where it can end."

Penny disengaged her arm from his grasp. "I think we both know the answer to that."

She turned to Antoinette and gave a curt nod. "Good night. I'll see you both in the morning."

* * * *

"Lark, you've got to help me."

"I refuse to buy you any more books. Every time I talk to you I have to exchange the old one for a new one."

Penny sighed over the phone. "Listen, I really need your help."

Lark must have heard the tension in her voice. "What's wrong?"

"Can I stay with you this weekend? I talked to the mechanic who has my car and he says it'll be ready Monday. Please? I just can't..." She sighed again. "I just need your help. Please."

"All right, all right. Stop saying please. Of course, no problem, anything. I'll pick you up this evening?"

Relief poured through her and it came out in her voice. "Thank you so much, Lark. I promise I'll tell you everything."

"I demand it." Abruptly, she hung up.

For the first time all day, a smile broke over Penny's face as her eyes fell to her bag at her feet. She'd had a restless night on the couch even though it was big and comfy. Thoughts had twirled around in her head. Even when she had fallen asleep, her dreams had metamorphosed into acting out her thoughts in odd ways. The one where Stu and Jed had been waltzing together while Kiley sang "Blue Moon" still stumped her.

The morning had been quick. Antoinette had slept in while she and Kiley got ready and left for the gallery; a quick glance at his set chin told her he was still angry from last night's encounter.

Penny hoped the weekend would soothe things over, so when Monday came, they could put this whole week behind them and have a good laugh.

Okay, maybe they wouldn't have a laugh. She definitely wouldn't be laughing anytime soon. Stu dumping her had been hard because it was abrupt and bad. Kiley would be torture. Scenes flashed forward to the future of her watching and loving him vicariously through work, an old maid thrilled just to be near him.

Oh god. How pathetic.

At least the work took her mind off all of it. She called Francois and pleaded with him until he agreed to have the car finished by Monday for an early morning pick-up. There had been no time to dwell on things.

It wasn't until late afternoon, around four, when lilting giggles trickled toward her, that Penny realized the last thing she wanted or needed right now was to see the stunning Antoinette and the equally stunning Sharla.

There they were, speaking French to each other and looking fabulous. Obviously the Parisians knew how to dress, and Penny wondered if that was taught in schools over there.

She had barely passed home-ec.

"Penny!" Antoinette greeted with a huge smile. "We came by for a chat."

Actually, Sharla looked like she'd rather be doing anything else. The woman was tall, as usual for a model. She had pale skin with long dark wavy hair, expertly groomed of course, with pale green eyes ringed black. Her makeup completely perfect, her body completely perfect...she really pissed Penny off, mainly due to the fact Sharla and Antoinette made a striking couple when they stood side by side, and that's how Kiley would look with the woman on his arm.

Hallelujah, the phone rang. Penny gave an apologetic smile as she picked up the phone. "Papillon. Ah, yes, perfect. Yes. Exactly. All right. Mmm. Thanks." She hung up and looked up at the pair with a plastered on smile.

"I had been telling Sharla that—"

The phone rang again. Once again the 'sorry' smile before saying, "Papillon."

And on it went for another three calls. Finally, when things quieted for a moment, Penny said to them, "Why don't we chat later? I see no end to this."

Antoinette's lip bowed in frustration but a gentle tug on her arm from the obviously bored Sharla erased her pout. "All right, but I insist, Penny. Sharla and I are here till Tuesday."

And with waving fingers they both left. Penny watched them with a sense of relief, not up to the task of socializing while feeling like a schlep.

The day didn't let up till around eight that evening. Lark called and asked if nine would be okay, and Penny assured her would be fine. Both had jobs that ran long hours. In fact, it was a miracle that Lark would be able to get out that early on a Friday evening. Usually, an episode of a television show took a week to film. Monday would start out with normal hours, but as the week progressed, filming could be thrown off by various time-consuming problems which included the actors' union clause that they get a twelve hour turnaround between shooting schedules. That's why Fridays usually were the longest days for the production team.

Whatever the case, it had allowed Lark to pick her up at nine, Penny wasn't going to question her luck. She had been prepared to stay at the office until midnight or later.

Kiley came in. They dealt with each other throughout the day in a professional manner, so she plastered on a pleasant smile and waited for him to say something.

"Are you going to lock up?" he asked her.

She nodded. "Lark will be here at nine."

He frowned. "I don't like having you here by yourself. Why don't I—?"

He was interrupted by Sharla, who had appeared all sultry and slutty in the doorway. She said something in French and gave a low chuckle. Penny decided, in that instant, she hated the model.

"No, I think—"

Once again he was cut off as Sharla grabbed his arm and gave a sharp tug.

"Go on." Penny waved him on. "I'll be fine."

"Are you sure?"

Penny only smile and nodded.

As if sensing his capitulation, the brunette bimbo gave a mighty tug. As they passed out the door, Sharla threw her a triumphant glance with her sea green eyes.

"Humph," Penny grumbled. "I bet they're fake eyes to go with her fake boobs."

She listened to them exit and heard Kiley set the alarm in place. She turned out all the lights and settled in front of her computer to look up some reading material. Tonight she wanted to read more about William Adolphe Bouguereau, a French painter, whose work with nudes had been quite outstanding. Her favorite of his, *A Young Girl Defending Herself Against Eros,"* was being housed in the Getty Museum. It had caught her eye the last time she went, so she had marked it in her little journal of things to look up.

Absorbed in her research, at first she didn't register the noise below until a large crash sent her heart shooting into her throat. Fear washed through her. Quickly she turned off her monitor, losing the last bit of light in the dark office.

Several things came into her mind, trying to rationalize what she had just heard. It could be Lark trying to get her attention that she had arrived. Maybe Kiley had come back. Maybe it could be mice? Ugh. They had had an infestation several months ago in the kitchen which still had her looking around daily to make sure there weren't little mouse turds lying around.

Slowly, quietly, she rose from her desk and made her way to the door, straining her ears. Logic told her if it were Lark or Kiley they would use the back entrance and let her know immediately they were around from the intercom. If she called the police and it did end up being little rodents again that would be too embarrassing. Of course, she wasn't going to investigate empty-handed.

She turned to the kitchen and looked around. Her eyes landed on the utility closet. As quietly as she could, she eased it open and pulled out the mop. She stood on the end and unscrewed the wooden handle. It was sturdy and long. If mice were anywhere down there she had at least a yard distance to shoo them away with.

She neared the bottom of the stairs when she saw the flashlight and fear froze her. Intruder. Someone was there, in the gallery, with her. She heard the unmistakable sound of ripping canvas as the intruder went through the displays of where Jed's paintings were housed.

She didn't know what to do. Her brain momentarily shut down. Her breath echoed shallowly through her ears. The intruder let out a curse as the sound of his knife became caught and his voice snapped her out of her frozen paralysis. She looked at the door, at the alarm and the panic button attached to it. There was one upstairs near her desk, but the door was closer. All she had to do was hit it and the police would be dispatched immediately.

Gripping her weapon tightly, she kept one eye on where the flashlight shone as she walked as quietly as she could across the marble floor to the door, silently thanking whatever deity was listening that she wore sneakers to work instead of hard-heeled shoes.

Her hand made contact with the alarm and a wash of relief surged through her. She'd be fine, she'd be okay. The police were on their way.

"Ahh!" Came the voice of the intruder. Penny jerked her head up and their eyes clashed.

He saw her. She saw him. He was a small man, a bit of black smearing on his face to camouflage him in the night. He wore all black with a small black ski cap on his head.

He had a knife in one hand and a nasty snarl on his face.

"God damn it! What are you doing here?" he screamed.

Penny had moved beyond fear. Her heart thudded painfully and she raised the mop handle high, ready to do whatever was necessary to defend herself.

The man moved toward her. Penny swung and missed. The intruder jerked the stick away from her and that's when she turned to run up the stairs, the only other place she could go.

She stopped breathing, and the only mantra running through her head screamed *faster, faster!* He pounced behind her, the swish of the knife making her cry out in fright. Suddenly, he grabbed her ankle and she went down.

The only thing that saved her, perhaps, were all the action movies she'd seen. She hit her chin, hard, but she ignored the pain as her body moved into survivor mode. She turned around and kicked out. The man grunted as he staggered backward on the stairs.

Using the opportunity, she scrambled to her feet and raced off again, this time making her way into the office where she slammed the door shut and turned the lock. She raced to Kiley's office, doing the same thing, struggling with one of the side tables until it rested under the doorknob.

Penny heard noises, but her teeth rattled so hard she could not differentiate all the sounds around her. The intruder was still out there; that's all she knew. She ran to the corner of the room and curled up in a tight ball, her arms going around her legs and hugging them to her chest tightly.

Only then did she feel the sting on her back. She reached around to her side and her hand came away covered in blood.

He got me, she thought dizzily. Her eyes crossed, the world faded...oblivion beckoned.

Chapter 11

In the dark world she found herself floating in, voices came to her. Kiley screaming her name, a pounding on the door. Shattering glass. Feet running. Other voices came and went. She didn't care. Here, the intruder couldn't touch her. Here, he didn't exist. She wanted the voices to go away and let her hide. She needed to hide.

Someone picked her up. She felt her body in a detached way, floating, being carried. Cold hands, shaking her. Her hair brushed aside.

Nothing mattered, she just wanted to hide. To sleep. She just wanted everything to go away.

And it did.

The next time she became aware of her surroundings, she felt herself lying in a bed, heard the unmistakable beep of a monitor and smelt the pungent sterilization of a hospital room. She cracked her eyes slightly, glad to see someone had pulled the curtains closed.

Kiley sat slumped in a chair next to the bed. He had on faded, ragged denim jeans, a plain white t-shirt and a long-sleeved white shirt over that. His hair was a mess, neither stylish nor even washed it looked like. A heavy tint of whiskers lined his face. His eyes were closed and his head tilted back. He looked exhausted.

"Kiley," she whispered, and he jumped, awake immediately.

His eyes took a moment to focus, as if wondering why he had been propelled out of slumber. The next instant they cleared and landed on her. Relief poured through his face, the emotions shining full force as he leaned on the edge of the seat and grabbed her hand.

Her other hand, she noted, had a needle in it plus a little device on her index finger to monitor her heart rate.

"Thank god," he muttered, and closed his eyes as his lips bent to kiss her hand.

She licked her lips. "Water?"

He turned and filled a glass with some water and helped her to drink it. The few minutes helped clear away the grogginess.

"Is Papillon okay?"

"To hell with the gallery," he growled. "I'm more concerned with if you're okay."

She gave him a weak smile. "My back hurts. And my chin."

"There was a...a cut on your side. And your chin is bruised." He ran a hand through his hair. "The doctor gave you ten stitches, said it wasn't that bad. God! He should have seen the blood, then he wouldn't say it wasn't that bad."

She stayed silent for a moment, thinking about the limbo she had been in as she sat curled up in Kiley's office. Scratches of information came to her like a broken, hazy projector.

"You were there?"

He nodded. "Security called me on my cell, said the alarm had been tripped. I thought you had left. It was after nine...."

"Sometimes Lark is late."

"Yeah, she showed up not too long after the police. I thought we might have to have to sedate her. She was hysterical."

"You found me?"

"The police told me there had been some paintings that had been slashed, and there was blood. I think...I think I went crazy. I pushed past them, not caring if I hurt their investigation. I saw the blood...it was on the stairs."

"He had a knife."

Kiley looked her straight in the eye. "The police are going to need your statement."

She nodded and tears welled up in her own eyes. "I know."

His hand cupped her cheek, being careful against the purple bruise. "Shh, it's going to be okay. You're going to be okay."

Penny closed her eyes, suddenly tired beyond belief. All she wanted to do was go to sleep.

As if sensing her fatigue, Kiley stepped back. Though Penny missed his hand, she couldn't even summon the energy to ask it back. A second later, she fell asleep.

There were nightmares, hazy images of a man and a knife trapping her in a maze, unable to find the exit. She tossed and turned and moaned. With relief, her mind suddenly realized she was dreaming, and that she could wake up anytime she wanted.

She opened her eyes to see a nurse standing by the monitor attached to her finger. The woman had very kind eyes. "Nightmares?" she asked gently.

Penny could only nod her head.

"I think I have something to help that," the nurse replied and left the room. She returned in a few minutes with a little plastic cup of water and a small capsule. "Here, this will take away the dreams." She helped Penny sit up and handed over the pill and water.

This time, when sleep stole over her, Penny dreamt of nothing. She fell into black nothingness and rested.

The next time she opened her eyes bright sunlight lit the room, and she lay on her side, a position she never slept in. She had vague memories of taking the capsule, and was glad the nurse had given it to her, though Penny had never been one for relying on chemicals to ease life.

She didn't have anyone visiting her or sitting in the chair. She noticed it had been pushed back against the wall. Her divider curtain had been thrown open to show she was alone in the room. At the foot of her bed, on the small visitors' table, sat bouquets of flowers of all colors and kinds. Balloons strained toward the ceiling with various themes like 'Get Well Soon' and 'Thinking of You.' Many cards waited for her to read, and all of it made Penny feel warm and loved.

A knock sounded on the door and the doctor entered, carrying some lab reports in his hand. A good-looking young man walked in, wearing a white coat buttoned up over dark blue scrubs. A stethoscope hung around his neck and a pencil balanced precariously behind one ear. He smiled at her when he saw her eyes open.

"Good morning, Penny," he said. "I'm Doctor Jack Carvello, but you can call me Doctor Jack. How you feeling today?"

His teeth shined big and white in his tanned face and it made her smile back. "I actually feel good, as long as I don't move my back or touch my chin. Were you the one to patch me up?"

"Yep," he said as he moved to stand next to her. He leaned down and took out a little flashlight to shine in her eyes. "I do believe those stitches you have are some of my best handiwork. My sixth grade home economics teacher would be proud."

"I heard there were only ten," she replied drolly.

He laughed unabashedly. "I see I have to be a little more clever with my lines."

He walked over to the end of her bed and grabbed her chart, looking it over and sticking the two papers he had come in with at the back.

"What's that?"

"You're toxicology results."

"I wasn't drinking."

He flashed her another big grin. "No, we checked your blood for anything the knife might have had on it."

"Oh," she whispered, suddenly losing her good humor. "I hadn't thought of that."

He leaned over and tweaked her nose. "It's a good thing we do." He wrote something on the chart before he replaced it. "You checked out A-okay." He stood looking at her, hands on his hips. "Are you ready for a bandage change?"

"I guess so."

"I'll be right back, 'k? Don't move!"

He walked out the door and Penny eased onto her back, careful not to jostle the bandage. She stared up at the ceiling as fragments of memories came back to her. The knife. She saw it glint in the moonlight as she raced up the stairs, but hadn't felt it connect with her. She supposed she was moving too quickly for it to have been worse. A coldness entered her blood...she had come close to dying.

Doctor Jack returned with a nurse, and for the next twenty minutes both helped Penny as he inspected the wound and changed the dressing. He assured her it would be fine, not a long cut but deep enough in one place where stitches had been needed. With his lovely sewing work, he told her, the scar should fade until almost undetectable. She assured him vanity was the last thing on her mind.

When they finished and she once again lay on her back with a bit of antibiotics racing through her blood, the doctor sat at the foot of the bed by her feet.

"The detective on the case is here, as well as Kiley."

She blinked. "You know Kiley?"

"I do now," he replied, and laughed softly. "He came in right behind the ambulance and wouldn't leave your side. He's very concerned about you."

"He's my boss," she explained. Though she tried to dismiss it, the thought of Kiley rushing to her unconscious side silently gave her a little thrill.

Doctor Jack nodded, though his eyes narrowed. "Do you feel up to talking to the cops? I can stall them for another day."

"No, no, that's all right. I want to tell them what happened, while it's still fresh in my mind. Too long and I might forget..." Her voice suddenly clamped up as her mind rebelled at the thought of reliving it. A cold sweat broke out on her body and she shivered the slightest bit.

"Hey," the doctor said as he grasped her hand, giving it a gentle squeeze. "Kiley will be here, sitting in that chair and I can guarantee he won't let anything else happen to you. You'll be great. 'K?"

Penny took a deep breath and nodded. Doctor Jack smiled and rose. He left and a few minutes later, Kiley poked his head in. He had a huge bouquet of yellow roses in a beautiful glass vase in one hand, and chocolate in the other.

The old Kiley walked in with a flourish, dressed that morning in a khaki- colored faux French military suit, complete with a cadet style jacket. To complete the outfit, his tapered pants were tucked into black combat boots. His hair had been slicked down in the back and a black beaded choker hugged his neck. He looked downright sexy, though the detective kept shooting him odd looks, as if he couldn't figure him out.

"You look good," Kiley murmured as he bent over and kissed her cheek. He placed the vase next to her on the nightstand, moving over another packet of flowers. Next he pulled the chair up and sat beside her bed. "There's color back in your cheeks."

"I had a dreamless sleep," she murmured, missing the frown Kiley sent her. Her eyes focused on the detective.

"Hello, Ms. Varlet, I'm Detective Malcolm Proper," he introduced himself, giving her a comforting smile. "I thought, if it would be okay, to ask you to answer a few questions about Friday night."

He seemed to be really nice. Detective Proper was a tall black man, with a very neatly-trimmed beard and mustache. He wore a very nice suit and shiny shoes. For some reason she had been expecting Andy Sipowicz.

"Of course," she replied, took a deep breath, and began with the time Kiley left.

Kiley didn't interrupt her once. In fact, he didn't even look at her. He sat in his chair, one leg on top of the other knee, arms folded, looking at some point down by her feet.

"I should have gone back upstairs to that alarm, but I thought the one by the door was closer. I thought all I had to do was hit that button and I'd be safe."

"We can always second-guess the decisions we make when at the time they seemed perfectly sensible. You handled yourself very well, Ms. Varlet. In fact, your quick thinking probably saved your life."

Another shudder went through her and the coldness came creeping back. The last thing she wanted to think about was her mortality while lying in a hospital room.

"That's about all the questions I have. Thank you," Detective Proper said, pocketing his little notebook.

"I might be able to help if you need a sketch...."

The detective held up a hand. "We actually have a suspect in custody, and if he confesses, which I have no trouble believing he will, considering, we won't even need for you to try to identify him."

"Great," she said weakly and closed her eyes. Would she have the stomach to look the intruder in the face? Her stomach rolled just thinking about it.

"Good day," the detective said and she heard the door click behind him.

She lay there with her eyes closed, forgetting Kiley was there with her till she heard his foot hit the floor. She cracked her eyes and saw him by the window, running a hand through his hair.

"I didn't know all the details," he said quietly. "Not until you laid it out, black and white."

"What did he mean, considering?"

"The police believe the assailant was hired to go into Papillon to destroy it."

Penny's stomach rumbling got worse. "Someone out to hurt you?"

She saw him shrug. "They posted that theory to me, but I can't think of anyone who would hate me enough to do this." He turned to face her and leaned back to half sit on the window ledge and folded his arms in front of his chest. "I haven't called your mother yet. I didn't want to upset her until we had more positive news."

"Good. She'd insist on flying out here, and I don't want to deal with her on top of this. I love her to death, but she can be overemotional."

She smiled, Kiley didn't. He continued to watch her with troubled eyes.

"Kiley? Are you all right?"

"No, I'm fucking not all right!" he snapped, closed his eyes and massaged the bridge of his nose with his first two fingers and thumb. "Sorry, I haven't slept. Antoinette has been taking care of the calls and helping, but I feel as if she's confining me. Her shoot is tomorrow, *tant mieux*, and she'll be gone on Tuesday."

"How's Sharla?"

This earned her a blank look. "Who?"

"Antoinette's friend. Sharla. Dark-hair French girl?"

"Oh," he replied. "I don't know, I haven't seen her since I left them both at the restaurant Friday night."

They both fell silent, looking at each other.

"What about Jed's show? What was damaged?"

"Seven of Jed's paintings were slashed." And he frowned.

"What?"

He shook his head but the frown only deepened. He stood suddenly. "Penny, I'll be back. There's something I have to do."

She nodded. "All right." But as she watched him walk out the door, a sense of unease swept through her, and it wouldn't go away.

Chapter 12

On Monday, Lark came to pick her up and take her home. Her best friend had called her several times in her hospital room but hadn't come to visit. She did her best to hide the slight disappointment of Kiley not being there. Penny had not seen him since his abrupt departure from her room the night before.

Lark saw her in the wheelchair that hospital officials said she had to use until her discharge had been approved by Doctor Jack, gave a funny little cry and ran to throw her arms around Penny, wheelchair and all.

That's how Doctor Jack found them, with Lark crying and babbling how sorry and guilty she felt and how she'd never forgive herself.

"She's going to be okay," he said with a gentle pat on Lark's arm.

Lark stood, turned, and threw her arms around him, thanking him profusely for taking such good care of Penny.

Doctor Jack grinned and hugged her back before disentangling himself as soothingly as possible. As Lark pulled herself together and blew her nose, he bent down to have a last word with Penny.

"You up to this?"

She nodded, holding the bouquet that Kiley had brought her. The rest of the flowers she had donated to the children's ward. "There's an elevator in my building."

"There's more to it than that, Penny," he told her, tweaking her nose again. "Those stitches have to stay in another week and a half, so nothing strenuous for that long. Try to keep them dry, so baths instead of the shower."

She saluted him.

"Do you have someone coming over to change the dressing?"

Lark stepped up, perfectly composed again except for the slight smudging of mascara under her eyes. "Me. I've already told work what happened, and the director, who's back this week for another show, had been so sympathetic he ordered everyone to make sure I get out of work by seven."

Penny to her hand in her own and squeezed comfortingly. Lark doing this for her was a really big deal. It showed just how much their friendship meant to her.

Doctor Jack stood. "This is for you," he said and gave Lark a small white bag. Once again he scribbled something into the chart he held before he handed her two pieces of paper. He gave the nurse the release signature needed to seal up Penny's stay.

"All right, you're outta here. Be back to get those stitches out and get those prescriptions filled. One is an antibiotic and one is a mild sleeping pill, just in case."

Though Penny doubted she'd get that one filled, she thanked him anyway.

"And Penny?"

She looked up at him.

"Your subconscious might be deeply affected, especially in dark areas. If you want, I can recommend someone to talk with you about what happened."

He meant a shrink. Penny frowned but thanked him, telling him she would think about it.

Lark helped her to stand and held her arm as they walked to the car, which had been parked at the curb with hazards flashing. Thankfully, her white Toyota was larger than Kiley's Beamer and she got in easily, if carefully.

"I have to go back to the studio this afternoon," Lark said as she eased into traffic. "But I'll come by afterward to change your dressing."

"Give me a call in case I need anything," Penny said lightly.

"Will do, though I think Kiley took care of that, shopping and whatnot."

"I wonder where he is," Penny said, very casually, but obviously not casually enough as Lark shot her a look.

"He wanted you to stay with him, but I argued that it would be better in your own surroundings."

Penny sighed. "You're right. Lovely as his buns might be, his home isn't mine. By the way, do you know when I'm supposed to go back to work?"

Lark shook her head. "I think Kiley isn't expecting you back for several weeks."

"Several weeks! I'm not that much of an invalid! I can still answer phones until my stitches are out!"

"Hey, don't yell at the messenger."

Penny let out a huff. "Sorry. I just don't want Kiley to get comfortable without me."

"Oh, I don't think you'll have to worry about that."

They had one stop, to fill Penny's prescriptions. Lark pulled up in front the apartment complex, setting her hazards on again as she ran around to help Penny to stand. She grabbed a bag out of the trunk and followed her inside.

The apartment was surprising very neat and very clean, and it smelled like lemon Pine Sol. More flowers sat on her dinette table and an inspection of the refrigerator showed it fully stocked with quick meals and lots of 100% juices.

Penny pursed her lips, grateful at the thoughtfulness, but wishing some orange soda had been left behind. Darn.

"These are for you," Lark said and upended the bag she carried onto the table, pushing aside the flowers. Books came out, about fifteen of them, all different. Some were advice books, 'Love in the Office' and 'How to Tell if He Loves You Back', some poetry books, a couple of art picture books, the last Harry Potter book, which she had never gotten around to reading, and several romances where the hero on the cover was blond and buff.

Penny eyed them carefully.

"Yeah, I thought they looked like Kiley too," Lark said with a laugh. "Well, I gotta go. I'll call you."

Penny enfolded her in a big hug. "Thanks so much."

Lark held onto her for a second longer. "It's the least I can do," she whispered, her voice suddenly growing husky, tears choking her up. "I saw you on the stretcher, you know. I thought...I thought you were dead. If I had only gotten there on time, I kept telling myself."

"Hey," Penny said gently, pulling back. She gave Lark a huge grin. "I'm A-Okay. And don't for one second blame yourself. There is no blame here."

Lark nodded, sniffed back tears, and turned toward the door. "Anyway, I hope those books help."

As she closed the door behind her, Penny picked up one regency romance where the handsome model on the cover wore skintight pantaloons, his back and likewise muscular buttocks turned to the reader. "I bet Kiley would look great in them," she muttered, opening to the first page.

* * * *

The rest of the day she took it as easy as possible, and enjoyed having a Monday off to sit at home and do nothing. She hadn't done that since high school summer vacation.

She did call her mom and tell her what happened. Mary Ann Varlet was shocked, upset, and ready to hop the first plane to Los Angeles. Penny talked her out of that, assuring her she was doing fine, that there was nothing to worry about, and she had lots of people looking out for her. Though her mother wasn't so easily placated, Penny assured her she could call her every day to check up on her if she wished.

After an hour, Mary Ann hung up, vowing to show up on her doorstep should anything horrible happen again and she not be called. She was upset by being left out, first at her and then at Kiley.

The books Lark had brought were a tremendous help. She was well into the regency romance when a knock sounded on her door. A quick glance at the clock showed it to be only five, too soon for Lark. Getting up from her comfy recliner gingerly, she peeped through the keyhole.

Jedidiah Yuki stood there.

Surprised, she unbolted the door and opened it, smiling. "What a surprise!"

Jed's eyes squinted at her and he thrust a bunch of grocery store bought flowers into her face. He swallowed thickly. "A woman let me in the front gate. I heard what happened," he said gruffly. "How...How are you?"

She accepted the flowers gracefully. "Sore but okay. Thank you, Jed, these are lovely." She brought them up to her nose. "I'm so sorry about your paintings, Jed."

Jed jerked as if scalded. "Don't be," he dismissed abruptly. "All that's important is that you weren't hurt."

"Yes," she murmured. "Would you like to come in?"

He hesitated. His eyes shifted around, first looking past her and then up toward the ceiling, until finally twitching with a nervous tick. Finally, he shook his head. "No, no, I best not. I just wanted to stop by and wish you all the best."

He backed away from the door.

"Are you all right, Jed?"

He nodded, a bit too enthusiastically, and a bit too energetically. "Great, fine. Gotta run, though. Take care."

She watched him practically run back the way he came, opting for the stairs instead of the elevator. How odd, but then again, he was a very odd creature.

She closed the door, bolted it, and headed for the kitchen to put the flowers in water. Most of them looked a little wilted, so she added some sugar to the vase, hoping it would perk them up.

As the evening wore on, she watched some television and read a bit more, wondering why Kiley hadn't called. He had been so attentive at the hospital.

But she kept reminding herself that he probably was up to his eyeballs trying to straighten everything out with the show, wondering if a show would still happen. Kiley had said that Jed's paintings were slashed, but she wondered how much damage Papillon had sustained. Sometimes thugs broke into galleries thinking there could be priceless artwork inside and when there wasn't, anger turned into destructive vandalism.

It made her sick, wondering how bad Papillon might be.

Lark showed up a little after seven, just as she promised, carrying a six pack of orange soda and sushi. Penny squealed with delight and would have jumped for joy if it didn't hurt so much. They spent a good evening together, eating and drinking and watching *Chocolat* with Johnny Depp, their all-time favorite actor.

Right before Lark left, she changed Penny's dressing, grabbing the white bag Doctor Jack gave her, which turned out to have all kinds of bandages. They sat at the kitchen table, and when the old gauze fell away, she heard a hiss.

"That bad?" she asked, curious.

"When Doctor Jack said stitches, I thought it was just a little thing. This...it's red, and goes from here to here," she used her fingers against Penny's skin, measuring about six or seven inches. "There are two butterfly bandages at the top and bottom."

Her voice trailed off.

"Don't worry. Doctor Jack said it would fade until you couldn't see it." She threw a big smile over her shoulder, hoping to ease Lark's distress.

She returned with a wobbly one of her own.

Half an hour later Lark left and suddenly, mental fatigue crashed down on Penny in waves. She turned out the lights and made her way to her bedroom where she eased onto her back. The pain medication had worn off some time ago, which made lying flat on her back too painful, so she rolled onto her undamaged side and grabbed one of her bears, hugging him tight.

She drifted off into a light doze, but nightmares soon plagued her. This time there was no ambiguous shadow haunting her sleep. The terror had a face, painted black, and his knife was very real as she ran up steps that never ended.

Penny's eyes snapped open. Panting, her heart raced from fear. Shadows from the corners terrified a pitiful whine from her and she reached out with a trembling hand to snap on the bedside light.

God, how long were the memories going to disturb her? The man had been caught. He couldn't possibly hurt her now. Still, her body broke out in a cold sweat and her mind refused to shut down, lest it surrender to the terror again.

She sat up and grabbed the bottle of pills, tearing off the lid and plopping the little capsule in her hand. She hated this even worse, this need for chemical substance to chase away the bogeyman.

She went to the bathroom and filled a paper cup with tap water, swallowing the capsule before thinking twice. Tomorrow she'd get on her computer and read about shell shock and how to get over the fear that seemed to cling to her in the night like a shadow.

Chapter 13

The next morning, she awoke to an awful banging ringing through her apartment. She opened her eyes, gagging from the cottonmouth she had, glancing blearily over at the clock to see it was near eleven. Wow, that pill had knocked her out. Even the bright sunlight pouring through her window hadn't jolted her awake.

Unfortunately, Kiley's awful music had done the trick. More cognizant, she heard him singing along off-key to the words she thought indefinable, God love him.

She sat up and threw off her blankets, using a hand to straighten her hair. She left her bedroom and hit the bathroom right away, not bothering to call out a "morning." She didn't want to look like a hag when Kiley saw her.

Fifteen minutes later, feeling better with her teeth brushed, hair brushed and bladder empty, she followed the smell of coffee to find Kiley sitting at her little dinette table, reading the paper.

"Good morning," she said softly, not wishing to startle him.

The paper folded down. He gave her the once-over, head to toe, not saying anything. He pointed a finger at a mug waiting for her before leaning over to shut off the radio beside him. With a grateful smile she sat down and picked it up, loving the heat through the ceramic.

"How did you get in here?" she asked after taking a drink of fortifying caffeine.

"I made a copy of your keys," he told her, "while you were still in the hospital."

She gave a nod of understanding. "I missed you yesterday."

He grunted wearily. "Too much to handle."

"Is there still a show Friday?"

Kiley hesitated for a moment then shook his head. "No, I've canceled it. That's why I didn't come by. I'd been on the phone all day."

"Oh, Kiley, I'm so sorry," she murmured. All their hard work.... "How is Jed taking it?"

He hesitated again. "I haven't actually been able to talk this through yet with him."

Penny frowned. For some reason, he wasn't very forthcoming with details. "Did the sponsors get very angry?"

"A few. Actually, the attack made the newspapers and the news, so most of them were more concerned about you before their money." He shrugged. "But I don't give a damn. This is why I have high insurance premiums."

"Kiley!"

"What? I happen to care more how you're doing. How *are* you doing?" he asked, looking closely to her face, which she knew had to be puffy from her deep sleep.

"Okay. Or I will be when I can get past the nightmares." She saw him frown. "Nightmares are to be expected. I'm going to do some Internet hunting today about dealing with it. I don't want to take the sleeping pills Doctor Jack gave me every night to keep the dreams away. That's not a healthy way to get past what happened."

Kiley ran a hand through his hair and she thought she heard something like, "damn him," muttered under his breath, but she wasn't positive.

His cell phone went off and he picked it up quickly. "Yes? Yes? I'll be right there." He snapped the phone closed and rose. "I've got to run, Penny, but I'll call you a little later."

She sat at her little table and looked up him. He cupped her cheek with his hand, his thumb moving lightly over the purple on her chin. Something dark and disturbing flashed into his eyes.

"Do you have a passport?" he asked her unexpectedly.

Penny blinked, bringing her thoughts back together, which had scattered at his gentle touch. "Um, yes, actually I do. I planned on taking a nice vacation next year to someplace exotic."

A ghost of a smile flittered across his lips. Abruptly he bent and kissed her, a full kiss on her mouth, firm yet oh so soft. It wasn't a romantic kiss. In fact it felt like it was a test of some kind, though what it could be a test for she had no idea. Seconds later he had pulled back and turned away, leaving her apartment quickly and quietly.

Long after the door had clicked behind him, Penny sat at the table drinking her coffee absently, noting he had moved her flowers to the living room, giving him room to sit in the kitchen. Really, her apartment was too small to have all those bouquets around. She had a neighbor two flights down who would be delighted with them so Penny picked up her phone and called Mrs. Shackelton who came immediately to collect them.

"Did your friend find you, my dear?" Mrs. Shackelton asked her.

"My friend?"

The old woman nodded. "A nice Asian man, he said he was a friend of yours who had missed you at the hospital."

"Oh, yes. Jed. Yes, he found me. Those are his flowers."

"Are you sure you want to give them to me?"

Penny nodded. "Except those," she said, pointing behind her. Kiley's roses stood there, in their vase, still beautiful. "Those are a little extra special."

Mrs. Shackelton winked. "That handsome blond fellow, huh? I saw him the day he brought your groceries in. Told me what happened. If you need anything, my dear, just call."

Penny thanked her and helped her load up her arms with the flowers. She helped Mrs. Shackelton into the elevator and pushed the correct floor.

"Bye," Penny said as the elevator doors closed.

The early afternoon passed quietly. Penny amused herself by spending half the day reading about facing fear and how to fight it, confronting it to humanize it. Most people who had some type of fear made it into a monster, supernatural and thus, unable to overcome it. By not hiding from it, fear became something tangible and thus, something to meet and have done with. It made good sense and Penny resolved to do that this night, finishing out the night without resorting to medication.

To reward herself, she finished up the regency romance, somewhere along the way substituting herself as the heroine and Kiley her dashing beau. The beautiful yet shy girl had discovered a dastardly plot in which the blond hero had come in at the last minute to rescue her, bring the authorities and arrest the evil villain.

Smiling, the phone interrupted her musings and she reached for it absently. "Hello?"

"How are you doing?" Kiley asked.

"Wonderful now that Charlotte is saved and Bronson has proposed," she quipped.

There was a momentary pause on the other end. "What?"

She waved at the air. "Never mind, just a book. Are you in your car?" She heard the telltale flicker of a bad connection.

"Yes, actually not too far from you," he said and she heard a smile in his voice. "So you haven't been bored?"

"Nope. Mrs. Shackelton came and took all the flowers, except yours of course. There were too many for this little place. I hated to do it, seeing how everyone had been so kind, even Jed, but—"

"Jed sent you flowers?" Kiley interrupted.

"He brought them yesterday."

"Jed was there?"

"Yes, he stopped by." The intercom door buzzer went off. "Oh, hold on, someone is buzzing me downstairs." She set the phone down and held the intercom link down. "Yes?"

"Um...Penny?" Jed's voice came over the speaker.

"Oh, hi. I'll buzz you up." She held down the door key for a minute than went back to the phone. "Kiley, I'll call you back."

"You have company?"

"Yes. Will you be free later?"

"I should. Who is it? Is it Lark?"

"No, it's Jed." A knock sounded on the door. "Oh! Gotta go." And she hung up.

Jed was dressed in the same clothes as yesterday, and instantly, sympathy welled up for him. As an artist, he probably had been devastated by the horrible destruction of his work.

"Come in, Jed," she said stepping back, wondering if her newfound knowledge could somehow help him out. "I'm glad you're here. We should talk."

She saw his eyes widen. "About...um, about what?" His voice came out high pitched.

"About what you're going through," she said softly. "Would you like to sit down?"

He watched her for a moment before collapsing at the dinette chair, great sobs heaving from him. She stared at him for a moment, her hands twisting together. Good lord, she hadn't meant to make the guy have a nervous breakdown!

She walked to the sink and got him a glass of water, bringing it over to place by him. She sat down in the other chair and waited.

Finally, the storm to smooth over until the sobs died away to hiccups.

"It's going to be okay, Jed. What you're feeling is normal."

"What would you know what I'm feeling?"

"I've got fear too. Every night I close my eyes and I see the knife coming at me. But I read—"

"You see the knife?" Jed interrupted, horrified. "Oh god! Oh god, I'm so sorry, Penny." He stood up and grabbed her hand. "I never meant for you to get hurt, I never thought anyone would get hurt...."

Somehow the words weren't making sense. She blinked and tried to organize them into some type of logical order. "What?"

"I thought it would be easy. That morning I saw Kiley punch in the security code...and he wasn't listening to me. I couldn't have 'Blue Anger'...remember? I just couldn't."

Penny yanked her hand away from him and stood up. "You...." Then she remembered Kiley's comment, that the police believed the intruder had been hired. "It was you?" He took a step toward her and she backed up. "Don't come near me!"

But he wasn't listening, he kept walking toward her. "I told him, just the blue paintings. I told him the code. I thought it would be easy, and with the work destroyed, Kiley would need my 'Slasher' theme. I didn't know you'd be there, Penny. I would never hurt you!"

"Get away from me!" She screamed and grabbed the first thing she saw, the DVD of *Chocolat*. She threw it at him. He flinched but, of course, it didn't deter him.

"Please, Penny, forgive me!"

She stopped and glared at him. "Forgive you? Forgive you! I could have been killed, Jed! That man saw me. He went after me! He slashed me, do you want to see?" She didn't wait for him to answer. "He was ready to take that knife and slit my throat, and you dare ask for my forgiveness?" Her fists balled up. "All because you didn't like the paintings you had painted for the gallery show? You piece of spoiled artist trash!" Then she punched him.

He went down with a heavy thump. The door burst open and Kiley stood there, looking like an avenging angel in black leather. First he looked at her before glancing down on the floor where Jed lay, her punch knocking him out cold.

"The cops are on their way," he told her. "Penny—"

"Catch me quick," she managed to mumble before joining Jed in total oblivion.

* * * *

"I wasn't supposed to see you until these were coming out," Doctor Jack teased her. "Not putting them back in."

Penny winced as he pulled the needle. She wasn't looking at him but she didn't need to. She could feel the pinch and pull. She was grateful for the shot of painkiller he'd given her earlier. At least with that she wasn't really caring that a needle went in and out of her flesh.

Kiley stood in the emergency room with her, watching and wincing with her. "You should see the other guy," he said wearily.

Doctor Jack eyed him and cast a look over Penny, reaching out and picking up her hand, inspecting her bruised knuckles. "Eye or chin?"

She shrugged. "Somewhere on his face. I dunno where it landed."

"Eye," Kiley answered.

Doctor Jack replaced her hand on her leg and pushed his chair away to take off his gloves, mask and eye protection, the standard issue for treating bloody wounds. "If you don't pop those stitches, I'll see you in two weeks."

"Actually, if you don't mind, I need to talk to you about that," Kiley murmured to him. "Can I call you tomorrow?"

"Sure." Doctor Jack nodded. He dug in his white coat and handed over a card that Kiley took with a smile and pocketed.

Ten minutes later they sat in Kiley's car. Penny's head rolled on the headrest. She wasn't ready to pass out but she was more than relaxed.

"I can't believe he did that," she muttered. "Jed. I just can't believe he did that."

"I had a suspicion when I realized which paintings had been destroyed, only the ones Jed had been insisting on removing from the show." He eased into traffic. "When I told Detective Proper, he started questioning the asshole that broke in. He confessed, but we couldn't find Jed. That was one reason I had been surprised to hear he had visited you."

"Why didn't you tell me what was going on?"

"Because you had so much else to deal with, I didn't think you needed this added to that list. But if I had known Jed's conscious had gotten to him...." He trailed the sentence off, not needing to voice the rest of it.

Penny sighed. "Poor Jed."

"Fuck Jed," Kiley's muttered.

"After this, his career is going to vanish. It's a shame how one wrong decision is going to cost him everything."

"It almost cost me everything!"

She bit her lip, yes...Papillon could suffer slightly from this. Had this happened to anyone else in the art world it might have been worse. "Papillon will survive. Your name is highly respected in the field, so I'm positive things will work out," she murmured but was cut off by a gurgled sound from him.

"That's not...oh never mind." He sighed.

They drove in silence for a minute. She looked at him, watching his profile. "Thank you," she whispered.

"For what?"

"For coming to my rescue."

He didn't say anything. Instead, he picked up her bruised hand, running a finger over the knuckles once before having to shift gears.

"I'm closing Papillon for a few weeks," he told her suddenly, but his decision didn't really surprise her. "I want everything remodeled, every reminder of what happened gone. While the work is being done, I've decided to visit my parents. My lawyer will handle the contractor and specifications."

It was not what she wanted to hear. The thought of going back to work had kept her spirits up, and now the thought of sitting around without that stimulus deflated her. Not to mention the fact that she would miss him terribly.

"We leave in two days," he finished.

It took a moment for her brain to comprehend what he had just said since the painkiller was starting to shut down some of her basic comprehension skills. Even after it did compute that he said "we" and not "I", all she could manage was a dumb, "Huh?" in a high squeak.

Chapter 14

"I can't go to Paris with you, Kiley," she managed to get out.

He patted her hand, almost patronizingly. "It's not like you're going to work with Papillon shut down."

She snatched her hand away, giving him a huffy glare. "I can't afford to go jaunting off to France, not that I'm complaining about my salary," she hastened to add. "But I have my car to pay for, rent, utilities...." Her hand waved in the air, as if going on with the list even though her mouth had stopped moving.

"It's two weeks, Penny, not a lifetime commitment," he injected dryly. "If you must justify it, think of it as worker's compensation."

She crossed her arms. "And where is that stated in the worker's comp bylaws? Get assaulted so you get two weeks in Paris?"

His fist clenched on the steering wheel. She saw the outer corners of his mouth whiten. "Don't you want to go?" he growled, but she rather thought that wasn't precisely what he had been thinking.

"Of course I do," she answered. "That's not the problem."

"I don't see why we're having this conversation."

Penny never realized, until that moment, how dense he could be. "Fine, you want it spelled out? I. Don't. Have. The. Money. Not enough of it right now. I have to—"

He cut her off as he began to laugh. Of all the nerve!

"Penny, did you think I would invite you to go to my home and expect you to foot your own expenses?"

Her eyes widened. "You can't pay for me!"

"I have already done so," he told her softly. "It's the least I can offer after what you've endured."

"But...but...Kiley, it wasn't your fault what happened! I don't hold you responsible!"

"Did you think, for one moment, that what happened to you hasn't haunted me every night?" He went on, his voice holding a thread of agony. "I wake up every night to the same nightmare. I see the blood...your blood, on the stairs, and I follow it. It's like the world has slowed down. I get to my office door and I know I have to get inside...but in the dream I see," he faltered, and cleared his throat. "I can't tell you what I see."

He stopped talking for a moment, and Penny had no desire to talk either, for she had her share of nightmares as well. She had a pretty good idea what he saw once he pushed open that door.

"So," he went on, his voice back to its normal mellow baritone, "this trip is justifiable workers' comp for me and, I suspect, for you. As for your car, Francois is taking care of it until we get back, no charge."

Penny didn't say anything more. She hadn't realized Kiley shouldered the responsibility of guilt, and if he needed this trip, more specifically a trip he needed to make with her, then how could she to deny that for him?

* * * *

They flew directly from Los Angeles to Paris, a twelve and half-hour non-stop flight, first class. It was the first time Penny had ever been at the front of the plane, and the plush seats amazed her. It was slightly embarrassing to see everyone walk past her leather recliner to the cramped seating of economy, but exploring her bundle of goodies soon took her mind off it.

There were earphones and Kiley showed her where to plug them in at, for either the radio or, once the plane took off, for the films. And not just one film, oh no, ten films on different channels running through the whole flight. So if she finished one she could switch over and immediately watch the next because each seat had its own television screen. She had found heaven for a movie fanatic.

She also got a nice eye mask, to help her sleep through the daylight if she wanted, though truthfully, she was too excited to imagine sleeping through any of it. The experience too surreal to miss.

A toothbrush, toothpaste, breath freshener. The oddest thing she discovered were socks. Really, socks. She held them up and wondered why anyone would take off their own perfectly good socks to use these. She rolled them up and put them in the pouch in front of her.

"So," she turned cheerfully toward Kiley. "I didn't see you yesterday."

"Last minute details. I called your doctor to tell him of our plans and that you'll be getting your stitches out in Paris."

"He said that was fine?"

"He sounded glad you were getting away, taking a vacation." He eyed her overly bright smile. "Are you okay?"

"I'm thrilled!" she assured him. "What else did you do?"

"I talked with Detective Proper."

The bright smile dimmed a little. "Will I have to testify?"

He shrugged one shoulder. "I don't know. Depends if Jed cooperates. It might not go to trial if he confesses outright. But, the Detective gave us his blessings on a relaxing trip."

Her mind wandered after that, until the plane sailed high in the air and she could turn on the movies to occupy her time. The week before had been the most puzzling, confusing and terrifying week of her life. So much had happened in the short amount of time and yet it felt as if had happened a lifetime ago.

Had it only been a little over a week that she thought the worst thing to happen had been Stu breaking up with her? Life had been turned upside down and inside out, and she thanked whatever deity had been watching over her that Friday night to let her still be here.

Stu wasn't the love of her life, so no need to mourn the failed relationship, end of story.

Distracted from her film, she looked over to Kiley, who slept, the free mask pulled across his eyes. His lips soft in repose, his head tilted to one side. He slept deeply, like a Viking resting after a weary battle. Even while sleeping he made her skin tingle and her heart pound. She half thought about asking him to join her in the mile high club, letting out a giggle at a mental picture of Kiley and her trying to do it in the tiny bathrooms.

Charles de Gaulle Airport was slightly different than what Penny expected. They landed quite smoothly, and were among the first people out since they sat way up front. But instead of walking into the terminal, they walked down a set of stairs to the tarmac where a shuttle waited to take them to the terminal. Very odd. Kiley smiled and took her hand, and she only smiled back and let him lead her. The airport was smaller than she thought it would be and the luggage carousel displayed prominently in the center. She handed over the international card she had filled out to the customs agent and passed through with Kiley, who didn't need to fill it out since he used his French passport. Their luggage came off early and he directed her toward the exit where he hailed a cab.

"Aren't we being met?" she asked.

He smiled down at her. "This is Paris," he said, as if that should answer her question.

Kiley conversed with the taxi driver and he helped put their luggage into the trunk. Both had packed little, though Kiley had an extra bag which, she had no doubt, held all his skin and hair products.

"I want to visit my parents first and then we'll go to my apartment."

"Do you live far from them?" she asked, as she tried to look though the dark to see Paris.

"No, right around the block actually. We're near the *Champs-Elysees*."

Penny loved how that rolled off his tongue with ease.

He chatted through the ride. "Paris is made up of *arrondissements*, sort of like area codes. There are twenty and go in a circle around the heart of Paris. The first arrondissement is where the *Louvre* is." Her eyes lit up at this. He chuckled. "We'll hit that soon enough. It's an exhausting museum."

They shortly pulled up to a nice street, brightly lit, Kiley paid the fare and organized their luggage out of the taxi.

Twilight fell as he punched in a code to a building, and held the door open for her. Inside the doors, a garden with a fountain and colorful flowers around it peacefully gurgled.

"How pretty," she said.

"Just be glad there's an elevator here. Most buildings don't have them."

They rode up to the sixth floor where the elevator opened to the smiling faces of Kiley's parents. They practically pulled them from the small cubicle, hugging and talking, in French obviously, so Penny just smiled wide and bobbed her head in a universal greeting.

Lilyane Laurent turned and embraced Penny. "Welcome, welcome. It's so good to finally meet you."

She had talked to Kiley's mother on several occasions, her mental picture completely accurate of the older woman. Lilyane had to be in her late fifties, though she looked around forty. Thin and shorter than Penny, she had perfectly coifed blonde hair and warm, blue eyes.

Her husband, Alain, matched Kiley's height, his brown hair peppered with silver, and laugh lines fanned from his blue eyes. There was no doubt that Kiley would look like exactly like him at his father's age, albeit with blond streaked hair groomed perfectly with gel. Penny bit back a giggle at the mental picture as they moved into the Laurent's home.

"It is so good to have you in our home, Penny," Lilyane said warmly as they settled in the den.

Penny gave a shy smile. "Thank you. I can hardly believe I'm here."

"Kiley told us what happened," Alain murmured. "If you need anything, please, let us know."

Penny nodded, her eyes darting briefly toward Kiley.

They all settled back and the talk fell into their native language. Even though she didn't understand a word what the three of them said, it wasn't an unpleasant feeling for Penny as she drank some tea and ate some sandwiches that Lilyane had brought in from the kitchen. She sat back and let the moment float around her.

But after her stomach had been filled, she let her head rest back, and the next thing she knew Kiley shook her awake. Penny blinked and sat up quickly, heat seeping into her cheeks as she realized she had dozed off on her hosts.

"I'm so sorry!" she said, mortified.

"*Non!*" Lilyane said with a smile. "We understand how it can be an exhausting trip. You are more than welcome to stay here tonight."

Kiley smiled at his mother. "Thanks, but I think we'll get going. You aired out my apartment?"

"Lucien did," she answered. "But I stocked it with food. Tomorrow, we must go for breakfast. *Oui?*"

Kiley nodded, and before Penny could formulate another thought, he whisked her out the door and down in the elevator.

"I'm sorry I fell asleep," she murmured, trying to smother another yawn.

"You didn't miss much," he said. "My mother kept trying to inquire, not too subtly, about us."

"Us?"

He threw her a sardonic smile. "You're the first girl I've brought home, and she's a woman after grandkids. See how it can be misleading?"

"Mmm," she replied. "I had my fair share of that with my own mom."

Kiley grimaced. "Too bad we're kids who respect their parents too much to say 'fuck off.'"

Penny laughed and gave a huge yawn.

"We'll take the next day or so easy," he said, eyeing her. "I suspect you'll sleep pretty well tonight."

The walk to Kiley's apartment wasn't all that far, like he had said. The entry to French apartment buildings blended in with the stores to the left and right of them, accessible only by a security code. He punched in his code for his building, but unlike his parents, no fountain greeted them. His door opened to reveal a set of stairs that went straight up. Penny looked around for the elevator but all she saw was a door labeled "*poubelle.*"

Kiley had already started walking up the stairs.

"Is the elevator up there?"

He hesitated and by the jerk of his shoulders she knew what he would say before he actually said it. "Um, my building happens to be one of those without an elevator."

"Which floor do you live on?"

Again, his shoulders did that little jerk. "The sixth."

She blinked, and blinked again. Kiley continued up the stairs. Penny stood there for a moment, realizing he wasn't kidding. She was going to have to lug her suitcase up six flights of stairs. Grumbling under her breath, she could only be grateful that she hadn't packed more.

"What did you say?"

"Nothing," she said sweetly, like arsenic sweet.

Yet once she got past the first flight that went straight up, she turned the corner and stopped dead once more.

Kiley gave her a sheepish grin. "Oh, and most staircases in Paris are circular."

She groaned and followed, knowing at least after two weeks her butt should be in great shape.

It took a little bit of patience to get up the stairs. Penny would go up a few and stop to catch her breath and wait for the ache in her back to ease. Kiley just went up and up, not even winded, and she realized now why he used that damn exercise torture device in LA. It was to survive when he came home and had to face this.

A few minutes later he came back down and took her suitcase from her, turning and heading up again. She tried to send a glower to his back but couldn't find the strength. But without the suitcase she managed to trudge along better and soon joined him at the top, ridiculously proud she had made it.

Kiley's apartment was worth the 112-step torture to get there. Big and airy, it had double windows that touched floor to ceiling and opened wide to let the cool breeze in. The front door opened to a huge living room, decorated in white and pale blue. Comfy couch, comfy pillows, large television. Her rubber soles made a squeal as they walked over the polished hardwood floors. Another spiral staircase sat in the center. Behind that a large kitchen, all stainless steel and white, dominated with a small dinette set in the corner.

"The bedrooms are upstairs," he said. "There's a bathroom through there," he pointed to a small hallway that led off from the kitchen, "and another joint one upstairs."

But another thing had caught her eyes. Paintings, various landscapes and the occasional nude graced the walls in warm colors. She knew, without asking, they belonged to Kiley.

"I'm so glad you have these here," she murmured, studying one nude, of a woman reclining against a vivid red velvet drape. The woman, whose face was obscured, was luscious—her breasts heavy and full, her body rounded in all the right areas where a woman should be rounded. Even without seeing the expression on her face, Penny knew she had just tasted passion. She could practically smell it.

"She's exquisite," she said softly.

"Yes," Kiley agreed equally as soft.

Penny wondered about the woman, but it wasn't a jealousy issue, never that, never for art. Kiley had captured something about her that made her come alive in the imagination and the painting stayed in the mind long after one had turned away from it.

She moved onto the next one, a landscape, and another after that. Each painting held something different, and each time she shifted her eyes between them, she saw something different, a different blade of grass or a different turn of the dirt, the strokes of the brush continually evolving and maturing through his development.

"Why did you ever stop?" she asked, turning to him.

Kiley pondered the question for a moment. "Because...I ran out of something I wanted to paint."

And that was all he said.

He took her suitcase up the stairs and showed her to the two rooms. "That one there is yours. Sorry it's not yellow."

She walked into the room and immediately fell in love with the bright, airy room. Everything was white: comforter, curtains, walls. The furniture made from pale oak highlighted the atmosphere. Large double windows lined one side and a vanity the other. The closet held the dresser.

"I love it," she told him sincerely before yawning again.

He flashed her a smile. "Going to crash soon?"

"I think so," she nodded. "It's been a long day."

"Why don't I fix us some food while you take a nap?"

"That would be lovely."

He placed her suitcase on the bed and turned to leave. Their eyes met, held. He raised his hand and with one finger ran it down her cheek tenderly, and in that moment, something passed between them. It was hard to deny the connection, like some type of silent communication each other had picked up.

"There are purple shadows under your eyes," he murmured. He tweaked her nose, spun and shut the door behind him.

Okay, so much for the connection.

Chapter 15

Morning light trickled into the window and onto her eyes, chasing away the odd dream where Kiley ran around Papillon naked with a spatula in his hand.

Her eyes popped wide when she saw the clock read eleven in the morning. She had lain down for that nap last evening and had slept through till late morning. She almost jumped out of bed when her eyes fell on a folded up piece of paper with her name on it.

Grabbing it, she read quickly, relaxing when Kiley explained he had gone out to meet his parents for a late breakfast and not to worry about rushing out the door. Relax, he wrote. Right, her stomach growled to remind her she skipped on food most of yesterday.

Penny rose and stripped off her clothes (which she had slept in), stuck the note in a side pocket on her suitcase, and grabbed a few things. She studied herself in the mirror for a moment, glad to see those purple shadows gone, half turning to see the bandage on her back. She would have to wait till Kiley came back to change her dressing but was glad the shower had a detachable head to make sure she didn't wet her back.

She took her time, walking from the bathroom back to the bedroom naked, toweling her hair dry. She applied her moisturizer before dressing, pulling on her ordinary costume of jeans and a blouse. She looked in the mirror and applied a light case of make-up. At this point she started to get excited about exploring Paris...Paris! She could hardly believe it.

She headed downstairs to the kitchen, planning on grabbing some juice to quiet the rumbling of her stomach. It took a few minutes, but as she stood in the kitchen staring at an empty bag and a plate with a croissant on it, she realized she wasn't alone.

She heard a discreet cough and she turned, screeching, clutching her heart. "Ah!"

A man stood there, within the open French balcony doors, watching her with an interested gleam in his dark eyes. He said something to her, in French, in a low melodic voice.

He was rather handsome, the opposite of Kiley's blond charisma in a dark and intense sort of way. Black hair tossed back carelessly, black eyes watching her. One eyebrow lifted as if waiting for her to say something.

There wasn't anything remotely threatening about him. He stood by the open window, holding a dainty tea cup in one hand, wearing faded blue jeans and a white shirt tails out with a tan zip up sweater over it. A nice looking man, a perfectly safe looking man, but in an instant, all that faded— the sunlight, the room, the cozy glow from last night. Gone. Suddenly, Penny was back in Papillon, back to being helpless. The intruder and the knife burst into her mind. Terror overwhelmed her. Only one thought slammed through the fog surrounding her brain...protection.

She spun into the kitchen, raced to a drawer and yanked, not finding anything to help protect her. Panic spiraled through her. She went to the next drawer and opened it, relief washing through her as she spotted some knives. Penny went to grab one in defense, but the stranger had beaten her to it, and instead she found her hand in his grip.

Fear washed through her and a desire to escape obliterated any other thought. She jerked and pulled, but the man's other arm came around her, encircling her, trapping her back to his chest.

"No!" She screamed. "Let me go! Let me go!" She strained, tried to jerk free, but all she managed to do was slide. Both sat down heavily upon the floor, she with kicking feet and wild pleas, he with a soothing whisper.

They sat there, for who knows how long, until the fright faded and the blood stopped pumping. Great heaves washed through her, making her gasp, but somehow her mind started to register the soft words the man said in her ear.

The fear died away, and the panic subsided. All that remained was a shaky emptiness that made her stomach roll and tears well up in her eyes. Finally, she cried. Great sobs hit her and she didn't even realize the man had turned her to rest her on his shoulder, his hand patting her head comfortingly.

She thought she was over it. The culprits had been caught, and she half way around the world. She hadn't even had a nightmare in several nights. Surely such fear shouldn't linger. But it did. Logic had fled her, even now as it returned to her.

The man must have the key, must know Kiley. He brought breakfast, had a cup in his hand, and looked perfectly comfortable standing by the window. An intruder wouldn't be drinking tea in the middle of the afternoon. An intruder wouldn't be dressed in relaxed casual.

The tears ran dry until a strange hiccupping took over. The man pulled back and smiled down at her, his dark eyes crinkling with kindness.

"Feel better?" he asked in a lightly accented voice.

She nodded, suddenly embarrassed. They sat on the kitchen floor in a tangle of arms and legs, his shirt soaked from her sobs and her make-up wrecked. Not how she had envisioned starting the day.

"I'm sorry," she whispered.

"Had the situation been reversed, I assure you I would have acted the same way." He held up one hand. "I swear."

Trying to picture him terrified, crying his heart out, painted a rather silly picture and brought a smile to her face.

"Good, you deserve smiles, not tears." He stood and bent down to help her stand as well, holding onto her shoulders until she seemed steady. He held out a hand. "*Bonjour, mademoiselle*. I am Lucien LeDoux, friend of Kiley."

Penny shyly took his hand. "Penny Varlet. I'm Kiley's assistant." She looked from him to the staircase, seeing the openness of the area. "How long have you been here, Mister LeDoux?"

He followed her eyes bestowing a wicked smile and an equally wicked wink.

Penny blushed and tried to look angry. Really, she really tried. But there was a certain appeal to this friend of Kiley's that made being upset with him impossible. After sitting here and crying on this man's shoulder while he comforted her, she realized her initial reaction had been quite fair.

"Please," he said. "Call me Lucien. Or Luci. I had no idea that you were upstairs."

"You must have heard me," she noted.

His eyes twinkled. "I had a vision I wanted to meet."

She blushed again, and until that moment she didn't think she had ever blushed so much.

His face turned serious and the twinkle faded somewhat. "Can I ask what put that fear in you?"

She sighed, suddenly realizing now what Doctor Jack had been trying to say about the need to talk to someone, someone other than a cop who wanted just the essential details. In all that had happened, she had never broken down, never shed a tear. It seemed crazy that she could cry over a non-important boyfriend, but couldn't over the thought of nearly losing her life.

While Lucien made them each a cup of tea, Penny went to the side bathroom to fix the damage her tears had made and brush her now dry hair.

She grimaced as she moved her arms, feeling a sting, and turned to the mirror as she lifted her shirt. Blood stained the bandages and she grimaced.

She looked at herself, took a deep breath and let it out slowly. Penny unbuttoned her blouse and set it aside and grabbed some clean bandages.

"Luci?" she called out down the stairway.

"*Oui?*"

"Could you help me?"

There was a moment of silence. She heard him walking and a second later his eyes locked with hers. He raised an eyebrow at her state of semi-undress.

She held up the bandages. "Could you redress my wound?"

He walked up the stairs and took the bundle she handed him, staying silent as he watched her turn around.

She felt his hands on her back, tracing over the tape and gently removing it, and she felt his steady gaze on her wound.

"What happened?" he asked softly.

"I work for Kiley, and there was an intruder at the gallery," she replied in a tone that matched his. "He had a knife."

He grabbed a washcloth, dampened it under the faucet and wrung it out. With featherlike skill he cleaned the area. "The stitches aren't broken, there's just light bleeding."

His fingers caressed the antibiotic ointment over the jagged wound before applying the gauze and tape. A silent moment descended upon them but it was a comforting silence. Luci placed his hands on her shoulders and rested his chin on her head. And strangely, she felt neither embarrassment nor shyness at wearing only her bra in front of him.

"Is this why Kiley brought you to Paris?"

"I think he feels guilt," she admitted. "But I hope bringing me here wasn't just about the guilt."

"Ah," he replied and she could feel the smile on his face. "I understand."

She pulled away and turned to look at him, a frown resting between her eyes. "That sounded condescending."

"I did not mean to offend, but I do see love shining in your eyes. So, of course, I understand." He picked up her blouse, handing it to her before turning. "I'll make us some tea, and we'll talk."

Hours later they heard the door open, and both Penny and Lucien turned their heads as Kiley appeared. He was dressed in khaki pants, a simple white pullover with a short sleeve russet button down over that. His hair casually brushed down and hung around his chin. He looked much younger than his thirty-odd years.

"Kiley," Penny greeted.

He nodded to her and she saw his eyes dart between her and Lucien. "What are you doing here?" he asked Lucien, casually enough to take the sting out of the words.

"Came to give you a welcome home breakfast," Lucien answered with a grin, "but I discovered this beautiful lady instead."

The edges of Kiley's mouth turned down, just a fraction. "Yes," he murmured and moved toward them. He grabbed Penny's hand and hauled her to her feet, holding her by his side.

Lucien said something in French, which made Kiley frown. Penny looked between them.

"Well," Kiley replied, "why don't we get together for dinner sometime, Luci? Penny and I are going out. Sightseeing."

"Actually, that's one reason I came over. I'm arranging a little get-together with some of the old crowd. I wanted to see when you," his eyes shifted briefly to her, "and Penny, of course, would be free for dinner at *La Paysage*."

Kiley thought for a moment. "We're having dinner with my parents tomorrow evening."

"How about the night after that? Around six?"

"Sounds great." Kiley gave him a smile that didn't quite reach his eyes. He turned to her. "Got your backpack?"

She pointed over her shoulder. "It's by the door." For great friends, Penny had the feeling something wasn't quite right.

Yet Lucien gave him an easy smile and said something in French, to which Kiley only nodded. He intertwined their fingers and tugged on her hand. She grabbed her backpack and a few seconds later they headed out the door, marching back down the 112 steps, all along the thought that she was going to have to go back up them later giving her slight heartburn.

"Kiley," she said as they went downward, "I thought Lucien was your friend."

"He is. I've known him forever."

"Well, for being friends, you seemed really unfriendly up there."

Silence.

"Kiley?"

He stopped suddenly, on the second floor landing. She bumped into his back and he sighed, reaching up with one hand to run it through his hair.

"Lucien is my friend, but sometimes I don't like him very much. He has this side of him that can be thoughtless. He likes to be...competitive."

She stared at him blankly.

He sighed again. "I was jealous."

"What?"

He turned to her. "I didn't like seeing you sitting so cozy with him, so close to him."

Penny was shocked, completely and utterly shocked. "You don't honestly think anything happened, do you?"

Kiley groaned. "No, of course not. But that didn't make it any better."

She looked at him, he looked at her. "You have no reason to be jealous of him. I mean, look at you."

His lips quirked. "Look at me how?"

She arched a brow. "Now you're fishing for compliments."

He smiled and stared at her with those intense blue eyes that did funny things to her insides, and it came back. That connection.

"Ready for Paris?"

Why can't he feel it as well? she thought with vexation. But she didn't say anything, only nodded. Really, though, he could have suggested they bungee jump off the Eiffel Tower and she would have agreed. That's what he did to her.

* * * *

He led her to the *Champs-Elysees*, through the small park that lined it, steering her west. They headed away from the *Arc de Triomphe*, after she crossed over and back at an intersection to see it directly. The best way to get the full scope of the monument was to stare it straight, except that angle lay directly in the middle of the busy road. Many tourists crossed the road to stop and take a picture and that's exactly what she did. The day was warm, sunny with big fluffy white clouds, a perfect summer day. People lined the sidewalk, moving like a school of fish. Tourist season was in full bloom and underway.

Though he was a native Parisian, Kiley took it all in stride, holding her hand as they strolled along one of the world's most famous boulevards. He pointed out little things, like how the *Grand Palais* and *Petit Palais* had been built at the same time for the 1900 World's Fair, and housed a major police department in the basement to help protect the exhibits on display. Currently the buildings were under construction with large scaffolding covering much of the glass and iron domes that made up the ceilings.

At the end of the street was the *Place de la Concorde*, a large roundabout, more or less, where Kiley warned her it was imperative she not jay-walk. Mostly, drivers in Paris tended to watch out for the pedestrian even if the pedestrian crossed on a red light but a few exceptions applied and *Place de la Concorde* happened to be one of them. He told her a funny story on how, when he was about sixteen, he and some friends, including Lucien, went to cut a corner to cross it and had been almost barreled down from two different tides of cars. Though he laughed at the memory, she saw the very real threat as they crossed across the large square.

Housed inside the square stood several interesting features, including a red granite Egyptian obelisk in the center that originally sat in front of the Luxor Temple. The tall column was decorated in hieroglyphics and adorned with a gold triangle cap at the top. In 1831, a French naval engineer named Lebas had been granted permission from the Egyptian Viceroy to take it. Five years later, it had been erected at the *Place de la Concorde* on the very spot where a guillotine of the revolution had stood. In return for the obelisk, King Louis-Phillipe gave the Viceroy a clock that still hangs today in Egypt.

From there, Kiley directed her safely to *Rue de Rivoli*, through the *Jardin des Tuileries* gateway. If possible, twice as many people walked through the pretty gardens than the streets. Circular ponds decorated both ends where ducks could swim and little boys could sail their hand-built sailboats with the aid of a stick. Statues of mythic gods stood on their pedestals watching with empty, scornful eyes. Of all the arts, she found sculptures the least pleasant. She did not deny the skill and craftsmanship of those artists who labored over the material of marble or bronze, bringing forth their imagination, but to her, a sculpture felt lifeless. No warmth or color existed in them and they made her mostly think of pious deities judging mortals through their sightless eye sockets.

They walked, taking their time winding around slower walkers or people posing for pictures. They passed several places selling overpriced sandwiches and drinks, past a pretty geometrically formed flowerbed, and up some steps to come toward the entrance of the *Louvre* Museum.

The building was unbelievably huge. Stone upon stone, gray with age rose straight up to form a 'U' shape. The courtyard was lined with ancient stone tiles where a water fountain bubbled high. Penny had seen pictures of the *Louvre*, of course she had, but photos could not give the breathtaking impact it had on first sight.

"Only in Paris could they have something so massive," she murmured in awe.

Kiley nodded. "I can't tell you how many hours, days, months I've spent in this building. My parents are consultants here, have been all my life." He tugged on her fingers. "Come on."

They moved on, Kiley waving away the street vendors who came up with postcard booklets, asking for money. The famous entrance to the *Louvre*, the glass dome pyramid, didn't quite fit with regal bearing of the stone lords staring down into the courtyard, but did add a touch of flair for the tourists.

However, Kiley being Kiley, they didn't head for the massive line winding in and out and around. Instead, he pulled her through an archway leading back to the *Rue de Rivoli*, to a side entrance.

In French he greeted the guard standing on duty. The guard smiled and answered back with a friendly wave, speaking rapidly what Penny assumed to be the usual pleasantries. Minutes later, they walked inside, going through a side hallway to emerge in the museum.

Penny found herself lost in paradise. All tales of not having enough time to see the *Louvre* had been absolutely true. The main hallway alone, lined with paintings, could eat up a day with her. And with Kiley by her side, talking about style, technique, color and composition in each one, hours clicked by rather quickly, under the works of Le Brun, Vouet and Friedrich.

Of course, she had a list of must see works: the Venus de Milo, Winged Liberty, the *Mona Lisa*. The *Mona Lisa* hung by herself halfway down the hallway, behind a protective case with two guards flanked on each side. A wooden barrier forced people to maintain a distance, and security cameras aimed on it. She and Kiley stood back until an opening presented itself where she could step up to the bar.

"She was stolen from here once," he murmured to her, pointing to the painting.

"Really?"

He nodded. "In 1911. She was taken by an Italian named Vincenzo Perugia who thought he stole her out of patriotism. He believed such a piece by an Italian should be brought home to Italy, but he didn't realize that de Vinci had sold it to King Francis the First."

"And thus it didn't belong to Italy after all."

"Correct."

"How did he get it out?" she asked, looking around.

"He had been a worker and hid while the museum closed for the evening. Since the *Louvre* was closed the next day, he hid inside and removed her by cutting her out of the frame. I think it took them something like ten months to get her back."

Gazing upon the painting was amazing. Not because it was an exceptional painting, not because of the mysterious smile the lady held, not because of anything really...except the fact that it was the most famous painting in the world. Penny had grown up knowing about the *Mona Lisa*, even before she had decided to make art her life. Words couldn't express the emotions flashing through her and Penny didn't want to take her eyes off it, not even to blink. It was a moment to savor, as if she connected to the artist of long ago. Leonardo de Vinci had painted it, and hundreds of years later, plain old Penny Varlet of Missouri saw it.

A silly tear formed in her eye. Kiley placed a hand on her shoulder and whispered in her ear, "It is okay, I understand." Suddenly it wasn't so silly anymore, to feel humbled in front of one painting that wasn't even her favorite. This moment Kiley could understand because he understood her.

They stayed inside, walking, looking, talking, exploring, all day. The crowd eventually started to thin out as they made their way toward the exit. Penny once again found herself on *Rue de Rivoli*, with the knowledge she now had to walk all the way back. She couldn't help the groan that eased itself out of her mouth.

"What's wrong?" Kiley asked.

"You're right. I'm exhausted and my feet are killing me. And now I just remembered we have to walk home."

"We'll take the metro," he replied.

It's one of the most important things, he told her, that most tourists didn't realize on how to get around Paris. The subway came in handy for moments like this, after a full day of exploring when the body was ready to drop.

"We did it the wrong way," he continued as they made their way down the steps to the subway system. "It's more important to get to the destination first and best to walk home to see the sights rather tire yourself out just getting anywhere."

The subway had a funny smell, a combination of too many bodies and aged dirt. Not a very pleasant smell, but it wasn't as bad as the walkways over the Pacific Coast Highway in Santa Monica, where the homeless used the steps as a toilet.

Kiley walked up to the window and ordered their little purple tickets, giving her a couple and putting the rest in his shirt pocket. Penny followed him as he slid his ticket in the gate near the hip. A second later the ticket came shooting up the top and Kiley walked through the turnstyle. Being casual, as if she did it everyday, she mimicked him. He sent her a quick wink.

Living in a city without a subway system—she didn't consider the one in Los Angeles because it didn't go anywhere she needed to go— actually traveling on it presented an interesting experience. All the seats had been taken, so she and Kiley grabbed onto a center bar as the train started off.

They traveled only a few stops, to the Franklin D. Roosevelt terminal, then transferred to another train to get to the stop closest to home. From there, she had just 112 vertical steps to relaxation.

"I know why Parisians eat so many pastries," she panted at the landing on the fifth floor.

"Why is that?" Kiley asked, not even winded.

"You guys need the sugar rush to face these stairs."

He laughed and held the apartment door open for her. "Why don't you take a little nap while I get us something to eat?"

She didn't even bother arguing. She made her way up to her bedroom, kicked off her shoes, and collapsed. She had almost dozed when Kiley called down to her. With a sigh, she rose and put on a pair of shorts and a t-shirt and went to do eat.

"So where tomorrow?" he asked as he set a plate of pasta before her.

She stared at it, a corner of her mouth twisting upwards.

"What?" he asked defensively.

"Domesticated Kiley," she shook her head. "That's one I thought I'd never see."

"No fair." He laughed. "I do have a certain degree of survival skills."

"And how many dishes can you prepare?"

He scratched his chin. "Fettucini, linguini, ziti...."

She mocked punched him on the arm. "I knew it!"

The dish, however, turned out to be quite tasty she had to admit, the sauce a nice blend of sweet tomatoes and spices.

He poured them two glasses of red wine and clinked hers. "You never answered my question."

"About tomorrow?"

He nodded.

"Hmmm. The *D'Orsay*. And Picasso. Oh, and I read there's a Dali exhibit near the *Sacre Coeur....*"

Kiley gave a half-strangled choke as he chose, at that moment, to take a drink. "So many in one day?"

She only grinned and shrugged.

He raised a brow. "What about the Eiffel Tower? Most people who come to Paris hit that first."

"Of course. But not tomorrow. Tomorrow is the *D'Orsay* and Picasso and Dali. Of course, Rodin if there's time." She leaned over and patted his belly. "Guess you'll have to eat some of those Parisian pastries to keep up."

Chapter 16

The next day Kiley directed them to the metro and from there it turned into a whirlwind day of art and walking. The *D'Orsay* Museum had once been a train station and the huge clock still stood inside amid the odd tiers that housed some of the world's most prestigious works.

Though sculptures weren't her favorite, she had to admit the Rodin's were impressive. She had been quite surprised, however, to discover The Thinker sat outside where nature and birds could have their way with him. Rodin's house was a lovely three story building with tall windows that brought the light expertly in each room to highlight his work. Along the garden path, a small restaurant nestled where they sat and had a bite to eat with refreshing coffee.

From there Kiley took her to the Picasso Museum, and once again, Picasso's work, though interesting, wasn't her cup of tea.

"This is nowhere near the work collected in Barcelona," Kiley told her. "That museum has a lot of his early work, when he did stills and portraits."

"Mmm," she hummed distractedly, turning her head sideways as she looked at one painting. "Is that supposed to be a turnip?"

Kiley turned his own head sideways as well, but in the opposite direction. "No, a girl. Look at it from this angle."

Dali's Museum turned out to be the last stop of the day, located in a quaint area in *Montmartre* devoted to the artists of the area. Kiley smiled indulgently as she pulled him to visit every painter set up displaying their wares for sale to the tourist population. Most of the themes depicted, of course, showed Paris and the highlights, but there were a few who captured more than just a nicely drawn landscape. It reminded her of Venice Boulevard and the little art deco pieces she had found there.

One young man, perhaps in his early twenties, rail thin with bad skin, had something that Kiley took notice of. Penny stepped back and turned her own critical eye on the paintings that portrayed people, in various ways of life and painted in various shades of white and black. The work wasn't the best she had ever seen, especially for portrait painting, as if the people in the art had bared their souls to all. But something drew her eye and if it drew her eye Kiley definitely noticed something more. He walked up to the young boy and spoke to him. Unfortunately, she had to wait till later to get a translation.

"What did you say to him?"

"He has style, there's something he has that could be brought out in his work. It's amateurish but," he shrugged, "I told him to call me."

"Where did he go to school?"

"According to him, he didn't study anywhere. And if that's the case then it's a natural ability which needs to be nurtured."

She studied his profile, a small smile gracing her mouth. "You'd make a great teacher."

He shot her a mocking look. "Don't get any ideas. I just think I could give him a few pointers."

Penny held her tongue, but she gave herself a silent bet she'd be seeing the young man art in Papillon's soon.

Surrealism was one aspect of art that had always fascinated her, and while Picasso left her confused, Dali's work made her stop and think. It gave a hefty impact in its statements. It drew emotions, and in art, that was the most important aspect.

Dali's museum was located in a basement, of sorts. They walked down a long staircase that twisted and turned and finally ended back onto the street. Very few original works hung inside, mainly it displayed copies, but it served its purpose of teaching the public about his work.

As they ended the day, they went to the *Sacre Couer,* a towering white cathedral that sat overlooking the rest of the city. The hike up to it had been breathless, not for the faint of heart, but worth every aching muscle it had taken to reach it. From the view one could see the Eiffel Tower and she turned toward Kiley with a smirk.

"See," she said as she waved her hand. "I saw it today after all."

He didn't even answer, though a grin tugged his mouth. He moved to one of the many steps leading up to the cathedral's entrance and went to sit, pulling on her hand to do the same. The sun slowly sank and the splashing colors blazed over the city, bathing it in reds and golds. The view overwhelmingly astonished and a left her a little bit in awe and at that moment Penny wished she had an easel and some paints.

"That's why there are so many landscapes of Paris," Kiley murmured next to her.

"It's the most gorgeous thing I've ever seen."

He didn't need to answer. He knew exactly what she felt. Really, Paris was everything and more of the expectation one thought of the city and she was so thankful to have been given the gift of seeing it. Above all, she was content knowing that Kiley sat beside her, sharing this special moment.

They walked from *Montmartre* slowly, both enjoying the end of the day. Penny was tired but she had dinner to look forward to. A few metro stops later, they were home.

* * * *

This time she was slightly more awake to enjoy Lilyane and Alain's company. Dinner was a relaxed affair, fish and vegetables with coconut flan for dessert. After dinner cognac brought light conversation as Kiley filled them in on their adventure that day.

"You'll have to take Penny to *Beaujolais,*" Lilyane said.

Kiley shot her a surprised look. "You wouldn't mind?"

She waved a hand. "*Naturellement pas*. This time of year it's beautiful." She turned a bright smile to Penny. "We have a little cottage right outside Lyon, in the *Beaujolais* district. My brother owns the vineyard next to it. You'd be able to taste the most delectable wine."

Penny smiled and nodded, afraid she might turn into a lush before the trip had ended. The French certainly did love their wine. "I've only seen the vineyards of California. Are there different cultivations?"

"Much the same, except of course, we produce a different taste of wine because of climate and soil," she explained.

Penny nodded. "That makes sense."

"If we go, can I borrow your car?" Kiley asked with a huge grin to his father.

Alain Laurent lifted his brows, sending his son a level stare. "The last time you asked that question my car came back needing a new paint job."

Kiley put a hand on his stomach as he gave a deep laugh. He caught Penny's questioning glance. "My cousin had just bought paint pellet guns and we didn't realize we had hit the car until several days later, when the paint had already dried."

Penny laughed. "How old were you?"

"Seventeen." He grinned at his father. "Between Antoinette and myself any car you owned had no hope, *oui*?" He turned back to Penny. "When she borrowed it she didn't realize lipstick could ruin leather. And it had been a very hot day."

She groaned and shook her head. "How did you keep from strangling them?" she asked his father.

The elder Laurent shrugged with dignity. "These things happen with children, and you must be diplomatic and forgiving."

Both Kiley and his mother burst out laughing. Penny looked back and forth between them, eyeing Kiley in concern as he doubled up almost rolling on the floor.

"He is a very good liar," Lilyane said as she wiped tears from her eyes.

"From what I remember, my *père* sat down on the street and cried."

"Like a little boy who had lost his favorite toy," Lilyane added.

Penny smothered a giggle as she pictured the older man weeping over a multi-colored, lipstick smeared car.

Alain Laurent humphed as he cleared his throat. "So *after* my temporary lapse of emotion, I did the only thing any self-respecting father would do. I bought a new car. And my children have never been allowed to touch another car of mine since."

Kiley, still grinning until he had the outright laughter under control, fixed his father with a level stare. "So, can I borrow your car?"

The older Laurent narrowed his eyes on his only son.

Kiley held up both hands. "I swear, no paint ball playing."

"And I don't wear lipstick," Penny added quickly.

Lilyane leaned over and patted her son's knee. "Of course you can borrow it."

Alain rolled his eyes but smiled widely.

"How are you enjoying Paris, Penny?" Lilyane asked, taking another sip of her wine.

"It's so full of energy, and I never thought of Paris like that. I don't know if I would have done so much had Kiley not been with me, I must confess, not understanding the language is pretty intimidating."

Lilyane nodded. "When Alain and I went to New York we only socialized with the small group of people in our circle, but after a while I desperately wanted new people to talk to. But it was hard because I didn't understand English."

"How did you manage?"

"The theater. I discovered off-Broadway productions and went almost every night, even though I didn't understand it. Slowly, however, it started sinking in."

Penny smiled. "It's like hearing how television teaches people English now-a-days."

"*Précisément*. Once Alain and I could communicate with everyone, I fell in love with New York."

"How long did you live there?"

"Three years. When I found out I was pregnant, we decided to move back to raise our children here."

"How did you find the name Kiley?"

Kiley shifted forward. "I think we should be getting back." He gave an obviously fake yawn.

Penny narrowed her eyes and shifted them from him back to his mother. "This must be a good story."

Lilyane chuckled. "In the play I adored, the main character was named Kiley."

Penny frowned. "But that's not embarrassing."

"Oh yes, it is. It's like being named after a soap opera character," Kiley muttered.

Lilyane just waved her son off.

"At least I wasn't named after a beheaded queen," he finished, smiling sweetly at the dark look his mother sent him. "Toni hates that one."

Penny laughed, trying to imagine him as a young boy, teasing his sister.

"Do you have any siblings?" Lilyane asked.

"No," she answered. "Only child. It was lonely. I love hearing your stories."

"Wait till I pull out the photos!"

Kiley groaned, buried his face in one hand, and slumped back into the couch.

Chapter 17

"Come on," Kiley called to her up the stairs.

"Where are we going?" she asked as she finished putting in her headband.

He grinned. "I need to find something to wear tonight."

"Your closet is filled with clothes," she said with a wave of her hand toward his bedroom.

"No, no, this has got to be something different. If I know Luci, there's going to be twenty people there, half of them I haven't seen in ten years."

She arched an eyebrow. "Black leather and zip up ties?"

He scratched. "Interesting. I hadn't thought of the goth route. I'll keep it in mind." He grinned.

Somehow that didn't reassure her.

And off shopping they went, Penny being led by Kiley, who seemed inexhaustible once he started shopping. Really, he seemed worse than Antoinette, but without the guilt of a size zero. The only good thing was that he knew exactly what he wanted. Some of the shops they entered had names like Armani and Gucci without price tags, but a lot of the times he popped into ordinary places that had something neat on display. He wasn't biased where he spent his money.

Though he didn't buy all that much, what he did buy looked smashing on his lean frame. Kiley had been blessed with a types of body that was naturally sleek, naturally tanned, with narrow hips and a rear end that rivaled Michelangelo's David. Really devastating combinations, especially to her libido. At one point he came out to model a see-through black body-hugging top and white leather pants...damn. When he went back into the changing room, she fanned herself with a piece of paper. Next to her the sales clerk, a short Frenchman, did the same thing. They exchanged bemused smiles.

Throughout the day he had stopped at various display windows where women's fashions displayed, pointing things out or making a comment. He would look at her and she would raise one shoulder, not agreeing with anything. The truth being that nothing was her taste. The clothes being touted were all bright and flashy, as if the eighties had come back into fashion. Bright pinks, neon greens, polka dots and lace. Penny shuddered just remembering her own experiences as a kid with such clothing; God, what had the world been thinking?

Of course, there was the other side of the spectrum, clothes only someone like Jennifer Aniston or Kirsten Dunst could wear. Cut made for someone without hips or an ounce of fat, which didn't describe Penny one bit. So the shopping day ended with Kiley having both arms loaded down with bags (and a suit) while she walked away with the apartment key as the official door opener.

Kiley decided to wear the suit, perhaps the first suit she had ever seen on him, which had been altered immediately in the studio. Though she couldn't tell Armani from K-Mart, she did know that the clothes had been made for his frame, hugging him in a deep plum color that offset his hair and complexion perfectly. He wore a black shirt under it but left the first two buttons undone. He had pulled the front and side of his hair back, slicked into a neat ponytail.

"You should get your ears pierced," she replied, eyeing him.

He tugged on an earlobe. "You think?"

"Oh, yeah. Very David Beckham. Very chic."

She, on the other hand, wasn't so chic. She wore a simple black dress that had been in style fifty years ago and would probably be in style fifty years from now, but would never be mistaken for fashionable. It was one of those little dresses that one owned for "just the occasion" and could be worn at everything, from a funeral to a cocktail party. The only thing she did differently was not wearing her headband, so her hair hung straight to her chin like a black curtain.

The restaurant, *La Paysage,* wasn't too far away, so they chose to walk. It was a beautiful night, warm but not too humid. When they arrived, Kiley talked to the host who led them toward the back into a private room. His prediction had been correct; Penny could see the acceptance on Kiley's face when they spotted the small crowd waiting for them.

Lucien came forward with several men and women, all greeting him with smiles, conversing in French. She tried to hold onto his arm but he seemed to slip through fingers as the crowd pushed in. She moved from the doorway to a discreet corner.

"Old friends," came Antoinette's amused voice. "My brother has been neglecting Paris too long."

Glad she had someone she could understand and communicate with, Penny smiled widely at Kiley's sister. "Hello, Antoinette."

The tall blonde hugged her. "How are you?" she asked softly.

"Better, I think."

Antoinette looked down at her somberly. "I wanted to stay and help, but Kiley told me he planned to come home." She shook her head. "Unbelievable, *oui*?"

Penny nodded. "The whole situation, especially with Jed behind it."

The blonde waved her hand in the air. "*Oui*. But I meant Kiley."

Penny cocked her head to one side. "Papillon?"

She fell quiet for a moment as she swung her gaze to her brother. "No," she replied quietly. "I've never seen him so shaken, because of you, not his art." She smiled and looked back down at Penny. "I've been bringing my friends to him for years hoping he'd find interest in one of them, but I see he's found his own love."

The heat hit Penny's cheeks. "Oh...that is...I wouldn't put words in his mouth," she stammered.

Antoinette raised a brow. "His mouth? Not yours?"

Penny looked away and chugged her drink.

"I stood on the balcony, Penny, and I assure you, I've never seen my brother so intense. We French know three things: wine, cheese and love. Really, it's written into law somewhere."

Through the evening she had a chance to observe Kiley, surrounded by the life and people that had made him what he had become. He laughed, he joked, he grew serious on certain subjects. Several times she saw his eyes moving around, as if looking for something but unable to find it. She didn't linger too long in any one space, didn't want him to accidentally see her being a wallflower and feel obligated to join her, thus taking him away from his friends.

Besides, this gave her an opportunity to observe him in such an atmosphere. During a gallery show she usually stayed upstairs handling the minute details so Kiley could be among his peers, and like those nights, he belonged to a certain class she didn't belong in. But these people were his friends, and somehow she knew her little black dress just didn't fit.

It was so blindingly obvious it broke her heart.

Antoinette drifted from her side, mingling. Another Laurent in the sea of bodies, both tall and works of art themselves.

"You should be out by his side," Lucien said softly.

He stood by her elbow so she turned to look up into his face. She had to clear her throat. "Why do you say that?"

"As his girlfriend—"

"I am not his girlfriend."

He stared at her with dark, penetrating eyes, trying to see into her soul.

She took another sip of her wine, avoiding his gaze. "We're just...really close."

No reply.

"Really," she repeated.

He finally chuckled. "If that's so then let's go to dinner tomorrow night."

Her eyes flew to his and she blinked, speechless.

He shrugged. "You said nothing serious, right?"

"I did not," she argued back.

"Not in so many words."

"I don't think it would be a good idea, Lucien."

He brushed a strand of hair out of her face with a soft, gentle finger. "What did Kiley tell you about me?"

"That you're competitive."

"So you took that as I have to have the woman he has, correct? That's not very nice." His finger dropped away. "You cried on my shoulder, Penny. I want to make sure you're going to be all right."

His tone was sincere, his eyes open and questioning her. She gave him a small, warm smile. "Thank you. You should seriously consider becoming a shrink."

His forehead scrunched together. "A what?"

"A psychiatrist."

He shuddered. "*Mon Dieu!* That shakes the very nature of my artist soul."

"What type of artist are you?"

"I paint," he replied with a wicked wink toward her. "Nudes. Would you like to pose for me?"

She raised an eyebrow. "Behave or I might say yes."

He laughed and grabbed her hand. "Come on, if you won't go out to dinner with me, let's get something together here."

She walked behind him, and something compelled her to glance to her side. Her eyes locked with Kiley's, held, and she saw his eyes drop to where Lucien held her hand. She saw a tightening to his mouth. A shadow passed over his face and when he jerked his eyes back to hers, something passed between them, but it wasn't the connection. This was something indescribable...dark, narrowing. While they still looked at each other, he deliberately turned away from her and put his hand against the back of one of the women next to him.

Penny stumbled. Though the moment had been too quick for any emotion to settle in properly, she suddenly felt nauseous. What exactly had just happened? Her eyes turned blindly to settle on the back of Lucien's head, and let them travel down to rest on his hand holding hers.

Lucien pulled her to the buffet table where she absently plucked finger foods onto a plate. They stood off into a darkened corner and ate. His talking helping her mind shift away from Kiley's behavior.

"I don't think you've heard a word I've said," he mused.

She sighed and abandoned her plate. "I'm sorry. I know it's very impolite."

Lucien dumped his plate on top of hers, and in a quick, totally unexpected move, maneuvered his body to pin her back to the wall.

"Luci!" she protested, placing her hands on his chest and pushing.

He bent his head and captured her lips. She tried to break it, but he had angled his kiss so turning would be impossible. She had to admit, he was a good kisser, teasing her lips apart with nibbling strokes, and sweeping in with his tongue. It glided with hers, coaxing, mating. She could feel the strength behind the kiss, and knew if he had wanted, the kiss would be commanding and brutal. Yet he held back, only teasing and flirting with her own. And for his mastery behind seduction, it left her cold.

Finally he pulled back and looked down into her dark eyes, his breathing slightly fast in the atmosphere around them.

"You see, that kiss made you feel nothing," he told her, matter of fact.

She blinked. "I think you should let me go."

He gave her a sad smile. "Don't let Kiley play his games with you, otherwise every kiss you'll have from now on will feel exactly like this one. *Oui?*"

"*Oui.*"

As quickly as she could, she pulled away from Lucien and decided to sit far away from him and the partying around her. She had walked over half of Paris and her feet ached in the little flats she had on. Besides, his little stunt had her feeling a little unsettled, realizing that her love life might just be ruined if this thing with Kiley went badly.

The evening dragged on. Midnight had just rolled around when Kiley found her and announced it was time to leave.

They walked in silence together, side by side, yet somehow a wide chasm seemed to have developed between them. Penny couldn't take her eyes off him, off his profile with his eyes down, watching the sidewalk in front of him. She couldn't tell if he ignored her or if he really didn't want to talk.

At what point did she lose the easy communication and friendship she had with Kiley?

Had sex really changed everything?

Kiley stayed downstairs that night while she went up to shower and go to bed. She waited for him, listening as he popped a cork on a bottle of wine and the opening of the balcony doors. The apartment fell silent. She willed him to come to her. She sent out silent messages urging him to come talk to her. She vowed not to fall asleep until this...whatever had happened...had been talked through.

"Penny."

His voice woke her from a light doze and suddenly he was on top of her in the bed, his body weighing her down. The sheets she had slept under pinned her arms to her sides as Kiley smashed his lips upon hers. His hands came up to tangle in her hair and hold her head still. She could taste the wine on his tongue and smell it on his breath.

He grabbed the sheet and tugged it off her, growling when he saw the t-shirt she slept in. One hand reached under it to hold her stomach down while the other ripped the shirt over her head. Something dark flashed on over his face, and it frightened her slightly.

"Kiley, what are you—?"

His free hand came down and covered her mouth, shutting off her question. The hand on her stomach moved to her panties and traced the mound outlined by lace before a finger slipped around the edge. She grunted as he pushed a finger inside her cunt, dancing over her clit. She had been dry and unprepared for the invasion.

As he worked his finger in and out of her pussy, a tingle shot through her, though it wasn't something she reveled in. This raw nature of lust Kiley displayed on her body held no love. It wasn't even wanted as the darkness of his face twisted his lips into a harsh frown. His thumb started stroking her clit and she could feel his hard cock against her thigh. In a dim part of her brain she realized he must have stripped before lying down on top of her.

He was ruthless in his attack on her pussy, and before long her body started to betray her mind. The small tingle from before started to build into a yearning and juices soon ran from her center, coating his finger. He inserted another finger and her body reacted like being hit with a bolt of lightning. At her moan of excitement, he withdrew his fingers and used both hands to flip her over.

The sudden switch of position jerked her from the sexual languor that that stolen over her. Kiley tore at her panties and they flew off her. His fingers grabbed her hips and pulled her pelvis up while at the same time his knees moved her legs farther apart. She felt his heat at her entrance and the anticipation of waiting for him to fill her up shot another tingle down her spine.

His cock head slipped up to her swollen pussy lips and teased them, up and down, playing them like an instrument. Her stomach muscles tightened in need. If possible, her pussy flooded even more as he pushed his way in, inch by slow, delicious inch.

He froze, one hand holding down onto her lower back and the other hand tangling in her hair to yank her head back. He swirled his fingers to secure them, and pain bit into the corners of her eyes where the skin pulled tight, bringing a soft sheen of tears to the surface. Yet instead of feeling belittled and humiliated, the ache traveled downward and brought her nipples to hardened peaks of pleasure. Her arousal was sharp, biting in intensity, and she couldn't believe how the pain, the pleasure, made her yearn for more.

Flowing from her breasts, the heat surged between her legs, a heat building until the throb was almost unbearable. She flexed her hips back, pushing herself more firmly onto his cock. Again they stopped to get reacquainted with feel and texture of each other. She felt the head of his cock swell inside which caused her walls to tighten reflexively. He let out a harsh groan before he started pumping.

His cock swelled in her, stretching and filling her up completely. He found a rhythm and followed it, a nice and steady pace in and out. Each time he went in he found that spot, that very sweet spot that made her shiver and salivate at the same time. Again and again he hit it, stimulating it, but never pushing it hard enough to send her over the edge.

As the pleasure grew, so did her frustration. She rocked back into his thrust, the hand holding her hair remaining still so each time she moved fine hairs around her face jerked. The pain heightened exquisite torture as he rode her steadily.

Finally, in desperation of needing to climax, her hand floated down, past the area where they joined, and grabbed his sac, giving his testicles a firm squeeze.

It was like lighting a match. The rhythm broke and he started pumping like a jackhammer, causing her legs to turn to jelly. He grunted, his balls slapping against her pussy lips with force. A squish came from between their union, and juices ran, saturating the sheet beneath her.

"Please," she panted in heat. "Please…ohhh…fuck me…."

He thrust faster, harder, going deeper and swelling to almost painful proportions. In and out, in and out, the hand in her hair pulling as if he held a bridle.

"You are so tight," he whispered in a ragged voice. "So fucking tight…I'm going to come."

"Yes," she answered. "Yes, yes, yes!"

The dam broke. Their bodies locked together as he erupted deep inside her, setting off her own orgasm with a wail of release. His thrusts jutted out of control as he slammed his rod with every jet, over and over, the heat triggering another one for her. They both fell onto the bed with limbs shaking from the force of their sex and hearts thundering in their chests.

He lay heavy upon her but he did not move. He released her hair, his fingers now rubbing her scalp in soothing sweeps, the rest of the tears trickling from her eyes and disappearing into the sheet below them.

He slowly pulled away from her, his deflating cock easing from her hole and letting all the juice flow out. He lay down heavily beside her, and though she really wanted to get up and wash off, exhaustion rushed into her senses and she closed her eyes in surrender.

Chapter 18

Before she knew it, daylight streamed into the window. She blinked and looked groggily around the room realizing Kiley was not in bed beside her. She lay there for a moment, replaying last night through her mind, wondering what had possessed him and why it didn't upset her. He had started out unfeeling, uncaring, but toward the end she had felt him thaw.

She rose, dressed, and headed downstairs. No coffee, no greeting, no Kiley. A heavy weight settled in her chest. How the *hell* did one evening change everything?

The last thing she wanted to do was stay inside the apartment and brood. Her mind tended to rationalize or contemplate situations far too long, making her want to scream. So she grabbed her backpack, the extra key hanging on a nail, and slammed the door. As she ran down the spiral staircase, each step seemed to pound out the confusion and replace it with anger.

What the hell went wrong?

She hit the outside and started walking; automatically tracing the same route Kiley had taken her on yesterday. Down the *Champs-Elysses* to the *Place de Concorde*, until she found herself staring at the glass pyramid that held the public entrance to the *Louvre*. The wind blew slightly and some of her hair caught on her lip as she turned her back on it and started to walk, aimlessly. She followed a side entrance for cars, crossing over another street, to find herself standing at a waist-high stone wall that overlooked the Seine River.

She thought the water below looked like raw umber, muddy and earthy in tone, with shots of cadmium red and lamp black mixed in the color palate. Low slung boats with tourists cruised by as Penny watched, her eyes swinging up to see the Eiffel Tower peaking over the building tops. Her feet started walking, taking her over a bridge and along the opposite side. She took her time, her mind curiously blank, for which she was grateful.

She noticed the *D'Orsay* Museum, but had no desire to go inside, so she continued. She saw the gold dome of *Hotel des Invalides* and ignored it. She continued walking until at last her destination towered overhead.

She knew the historical facts of the Eiffel Tower, built in 1887 to be the world's tallest structure, and how it had been saved by turning it into a radio tower in the early twentieth century. And like the *Mona Lisa*, this national landmark lived up to the hype. It towered, soaring into the blue sky as if trying to touch the clouds. Painted a dowdy brown, it had elevators moving up and down for visitors to get a bird's eye view of the city. The lines for tickets wove in and about, but seemed to be moving reasonably, so Penny crossed *Quai Branly* road to join the lines.

Various souvenir sellers came up to show her things: miniature Eiffel Towers, postcards, key chains. She shook her head, waved them on, and shuffled forward in line.

As she moved into the elevator, she couldn't help but feel sad that Kiley wasn't beside her. What fun could be found in the world's most romantic city when the person you loved didn't want to be with you?

She watched out the elevator car window, the ground diminishing and the city springing out before her. The Tower had three tiers, and people could get out at each stop if they paid for all three. Penny decided to ride straight to the top, not wanting to bother with the minor stops.

A steel, cage-type netting encased the top for protection but it didn't hinder the view at all. The tourists were thick, but that didn't really bother Penny either. She rested her fingers through the fence, watching the *Seine*, noting how the sun made the waves look like tiny reflecting mirrors. She felt peaceful staring over the city, even with the masses crushing her slightly against the metal cage.

The wind blew fiercely and she removed her headband. Her hair whipped around but it felt good. It cleared her head. Suddenly, a thousand plus feet in the sky, her mind cleared of everything. The nagging doubts since that night of Thai food and black leather pants, the fear of rejection, the recriminations of sleeping with the boss...gone. Only one thing remained: how could loving Kiley be wrong? More importantly, why should she deny something that felt so wonderful?

Love, like life, was rare and very precious and when you had it nothing else should belittle it. Not doubts, not fears and certainly not what-ifs. The revelation was so simple she wondered why it taken her so long to realize it. And it made her happy, too happy to be in such a crush so she made her way back to the elevator and rode it down until she found herself on the ground again. Under the Eiffel Tower she spotted a decorative circle of rocks, and headed across the small field discovering a metal disk and as she looked up she realized she stood directly underneath, looking at the belly of the Tower.

What a memory to have, what a day to have. She stood for a minute staring up the Eiffel Tower, feeling the moment far too surreal to ever forget. With a smile, she took off through the horde of tourists and souvenir vendors, crossing a little street to enter a park where kids played soccer. She watched them absently as she sat on a bench, resting her feet a bit from the long walk and the walk that she had to make home.

The day shone bright and sunny and it fed her happiness. How long she sat there she didn't know, but she felt reluctant to leave the little park, to leave the warm glow. She had just been given an inner freedom, her emotions had just been released, and she wanted some time to savor it.

But even the most peaceful times must come to an end, and when that moment came, Penny didn't mourn when she decided to find her way back to the apartment.

Her feet stepped over another dog mess...really, the Parisians did not like picking up after their pets...as she followed the same path home. Her mind started replaying the past year in her head, from the time she had interviewed with Kiley to the present. And for the first time, in a long time, she felt completely at peace.

Chapter 19

"Where have you been?" Kiley asked as soon as she pushed open the apartment door.

"Exploring. Walking. Out," she stated as if she needed to clarify.

His eyes narrowed. "Alone?" he bit out.

A curious sensation hit her chest. "Yes, alone. Who else would I be with?"

He ran a hand though his hair before pouring more wine into his half-empty glass. She took note of the empty bottle beside his opened one. "I was worried about you. You've been gone for hours."

She shrugged one shoulder. "I took my time. You didn't answer me, Kiley. Who did you expect me to be with?"

He swirled his wine, downed half of it and placed the goblet on the counter with a click. "I thought...maybe...Luci."

Penny held her breath, knowing this conversation would make or break their relationship. "Is he what this is all about?"

"What do you mean?" He hedged, frowning.

"Last night."

"Last night you were holding his hand," he snapped.

She regarded him calmly, letting his anger wash over her. "No, he dragged me to the buffet table to get some food...after I rejected his dinner invitation."

His eyes jerked to hers, searching them intently. "Rejected?"

"Of course I rejected him. I don't want to go on a date with him, Kiley."

Whatever he saw in her eyes...truth, simple honesty...it must have convinced him, because he gave a low groan in his throat and grabbed her arms to haul her into his.

He buried his face in her neck. "*Sacre bleu,* I'm so sorry. I just couldn't handle it. Not a second time."

Her hands reached up to hug him back. "Second time?" she murmured.

He was silent for a long moment, seeming content to just hold her. Finally, he pulled back. "You once asked me if I had ever been in love," he said.

"I remember."

He nodded, and she knew he gave more than an affirmation. "I was young, nineteen, twenty, around that age. She was a beautiful woman, a painter's model. It was a very classical, typical passion of youth."

"Love is never typical."

Kiley only smiled and tweaked her nose. "I figured you'd say something like that."

"What happened?"

The smile faded. "Another painter caught her eye."

Penny frowned. "Lucien?"

Kiley nodded. "It wasn't his fault, but I was hurt all the same. Angry. He was my best friend, knew how I felt about her and still made his move. What do you do in a situation when the woman you love loves someone else?"

"What did you do?"

"I went to study in America."

"Oh," Penny said.

"When I saw you last night, when I saw him holding your hand...I was furious."

The question presented itself so she had to ask. "Why?"

And asking that simple question made him blink.

"You sound as if you were jealous," she continued, and she had to shush the little voice reminding her that her heart pumped madly.

He ran a hand through his hair. "If I did, I didn't mean to make you feel uncomfortable."

If she had been hoping for a declaration she tried not to let the disappointment show. She gave a point to the wall over her shoulder without breaking eye contact. "It was her, wasn't it?"

"Yes," he answered softly. "But that's not why I keep it on my wall. It's a fucking great piece of work."

The serious mood instantly shattered and a smile crept forward to curl her lips.

"Let's go on a trip together," he said suddenly.

"We are on a trip together."

"No. Let's go to *Beaujolais*. We'll spend a few days there. Our cottage has a pool. It's quiet, nothing to interrupt us."

She quirked an eyebrow. "Sounds...romantic."

The smile he gave her was lethal. His eyes lit up with a cunning light that suggested romance might only be part of his idea.

* * * *

She repacked her suitcase the next morning and lugged it down the six flights of stairs, trying not to think how she would have to come back up in a few days.

Kiley waited out front in front of his father's car, a Mercedes sedan, and raised his brow when he saw the suitcase. "We're only going for a few days."

"I know that," she replied patiently. "But we're going to a place I've no idea what to expect. I don't want to do one of those wish-I-had-brought-that routines."

Sometimes men could be extremely dense.

* * * *

Paris did not show what France was really like. The capitol was a mecca of art, fashion, and life in general. A city that rarely slept and invited all to experience what living could really be about, along with the freedom to explore anything. If you walked away from Paris bored or full of negativity then you never really understood the message it tried to teach you.

But the countryside was the complete opposite. It had green hills, spattered with towns, castles that rose in the horizon, and the grace of an old world. Once the rough outskirts of the city fell away, Penny came down with a bit of nostalgia.

"It reminds me of Missouri," she murmured.

"What does?"

"The country, even the cows. It's just hills that roll on as far as the eye can see, flat and yet dancing in the wind on invisible strings."

Kiley didn't say anything. He rolled the windows down, turning off the air conditioning. He slipped in some music, something along his taste of music with a hard bass and soulful singer. The music, however, fit in with the adventure so Penny laughed and stuck her hand out to feel the wind against her skin. Warm, vibrant, her hair blew back from her face as she laughed.

They headed south, toward a little village called *Jaune-sur-Coteau*, near Lyon, where he and Antoinette had spent many a summer as children, and where he had painted his first painting, at the tender age of five. "My mother still has that painting," he laughed, shaking his head. "She framed it and hung up at the cottage."

Late afternoon they entered a small village which had half a dozen narrow streets, a very large church in the town center, three pubs across from it, and various odd shops. Kiley pulled into an unlined parking spot and cut the engine.

They got out of the car and Penny turned in a circle to take in the peaceful atmosphere: the dropping tress, an old couple feeding the birds in front of the church, dogs barking in the distance. She also noticed only three cars parked in front of the pub, theirs being one.

The church, the bars, and all the houses seemed to be made with the same tan colored stone that reminded her of pictures of little homes built from earthen baked clay, like how the prairie settlers had used dried mud to give them shelter. Only one or two buildings were wooden, or mortared brick.

"What do you think?" Kiley asked her, sweeping a hand around the quaint little town.

"I don't think I've actually been to a town where every building was the same color."

Kiley grinned. "There's some type of natural stone deposit nearby, hence the building material. Come on." He waved to her and walked toward the first pub.

As they stepped into the small bar, a cheer and round of greetings rushed at them. Penny watched a grin light up Kiley's face as several of the patrons came up to hug him. Kiley hugged each man and kissed on both cheeks. He spoke in French, greeting all, and pulled her to his side.

Penny smiled, even when the Frenchmen came up and gave her the same greeting as a hug and kissed cheeks, speaking to her as if she understood them. She just nodded and she supposed this plan worked because they seemed satisfied. He gave a little wave and pulled her past the bar through a side door and into a dining room.

The few diners eating called out greetings, but refrained from jumping to their feet and leaving their food. She had learned from first hand experience that the French were very loyal to their meals. The hostess was a young girl and, Penny guessed, didn't know Kiley very well, as there were no squeals or kissing. She led them to a table in the back, near the window, giving them a view of the rolling hillside.

Kiley ordered without looking at the menu. In fact, there weren't any menus that Penny could notice.

"Is there a restroom?" she asked him.

He pointed to a door. "But look to the right as you walk in," he told her.

That made her pause midway in rising. "Why?" she asked suspiciously.

But he only gave her a shrug, smiled innocently, and gestured again to the door. So she went, but not without some trepidation. And as she pushed open the door, making sure to keep her eyes to the right, she understood. It was a unisex bathroom, though luckily no one stood at the urinals located on the left, right in front of the women's stalls. And this was no *Ally McBeal* set. The urinals lined the wall right out in public, for anyone to see anything that exposed and being used. And to top it off, a public phone right hung next to the first urinal.

Closing her eyes and shaking her head, knowing Kiley sat at the table laughing, she hurried to one of the stalls. The only thing she could be thankful for was the fact the stall had a door for her to keep *her* privates private.

Several minutes later she reemerged at the table, having to wait a few seconds when she heard someone come in and use the urinals, refusing to be liberated enough to see a strange man relieving himself and be nonchalant.

"Well, what an experience," she announced as she sat down, noticing a glass of white wine had been placed in front of her setting. She picked it up and took a hefty sip.

"I thought you might find that amusing."

"I can't wait to tell Lark about that," she said, shaking her head. "Are all the restrooms here like that?"

"The French have a very liberal attitude on these things," he told her, and she noticed a devilish twinkle in his blue eyes.

"About peeing in front of one another? Listen, men might be liberal about that stuff since they do it all the time," she leaned in a bit closer and lowered her voice, "measuring each others endowments."

Kiley sputtered on the sip of wine he had just taken.

"But women," she finished, "like a spot of privacy."

He laughed and continued to chuckle periodically through one of most delicious meals she had ever eaten. He had ordered salmon for her and a filet mignon for himself, with a side of potatoes au gratin. He ordered a flan as dessert for both, rich and creamy that complemented their wine.

"This is really good," she said as he emptied the bottle into her glass.

"Thanks," he said.

She picked up the bottle and looked at the label. "Your family's?"

He nodded. "My uncle, Henri Macreaux, my mother's older brother. I have some cousins around here somewhere."

"Is that where we're staying?"

"No. My parents have their own cottage." He finished his glass of wine. "Ready to go?"

She nodded and stood, leading the way back they had come. Kiley left money on the table and they walked back into the pub, going through the cheers and greetings again, and receiving several more kisses.

She smiled, feeling slightly tipsy as she settled back into the Mercedes. "That was amazing."

"The food?"

She waved her hand. "All of it. Everyone knew you."

"Well, I might have been more of a hellion as a child then I let on." He laughed. "The owner of that place is a nice man named Gerald, and more than one occasion I remember him slapping my hand with a stick as I tried to steal the pastries he had out for sale."

"Shame on you," she teased.

He shook his head. "When he finds out I'm back in town, he's going to take away all his sweets."

They drove through the darkening streets of the village, over the cobblestone road, and out into the countryside. The streets weren't big enough for two vehicles and once Kiley had to pull onto the grass to let another car pass. He made a sharp turn farther down and soon they rolled through a gate and up to a large chateau, complete with plantation style steps, pillars, and a large pool out front.

"What is this?"

"The cottage."

She turned an incredulous eye on him as he braked the car. "Please don't tell me you consider this a cottage, Kiley." She waved at the large structure. "This is a fucking mansion!"

"You think? Come on then, let us see the mansion." He smiled as he popped the trunk and left the car.

She sat for a moment in the passenger seat, shaking her head, until he tapped on her window and beckoned her to follow. And of course, there were servants, an older couple who greeted them as Kiley finished hauling up her suitcase up the front steps, panting slightly.

"Penny, this is *Madame* and *Monsieur* Mourre," he introduced.

Penny smiled at them and greeted them in the only French word she knew. "*Bonjour*," to which they chuckled.

"*Bonsoir*," they said.

Penny looked at Kiley. "Good evening," he translated.

"Oh," she said, "right. *Bonsoir*."

The chateau felt like a palace inside, huge with marble tiles, French provincial furniture and paintings of dour-looking people in white powdered wigs. Everything lit with a soft glow, making it seem even more gilded. The Mourres took them out of the main foyer and up the stairs and everything changed. The top of the staircase had made a "T" formation, and they turned to the right. The long hallway she found herself walking in had numerous windows lining it. This hallway led to several rooms she sneaked peaks at, and found that the ascetic decor turned into a warm and cheerful mess of mismatched furniture, childish framed drawings, throw rugs and warm tones. It became a home instead of an ostentatious showroom.

"I don't know why my parents keep that stuff in the foyer," Kiley said, catching her shocked expression. "Appearance, I suppose, though I don't know who they're trying to impress. No one ever comes here except family."

Several of the rooms were the kind of room she had always labeled "junk rooms," which meant they really served no purpose other than storing stuff deemed too sentimental to throw away. Madame Mourre's kept the room neatly arranged and nicely organized.

Another room, a larger room, had toys. Penny had to stop and stare at the rocking horse she saw.

"That was mine," Kiley said.

She looked at him in surprise. "You still have your childhood rocking chair?"

He shrugged. "Not me, my mother. Said she wanted to save it for my kids."

Penny laughed.

Getting to their bedrooms became a joke, as they had to take two different hallways to find where they were located. Kiley's room boasted a multitude of colors: greens, reds, browns. Nothing really matched, but it held a large bed that looked fluffy. Her own bedroom had been painted a brown on beige motif, with several large ferns in the corners. All that seemed to be missing was a mosquito net around the bed for the African safari feel.

As she unpacked her suitcase, she heard Kiley talking to the Mourres before walking into her room several minutes later. He changed from his traveling clothes, white linen pants and a gauzy, black Indian style shirt, into very baggy jeans and an equally baggy shirt. He sat on her bed, watching her, mindful to keep his running shoes off her comforter.

"What?" she asked, after a few minutes of him looking at her.

"Want to go try some fresh wine?"

"At your uncle's?"

"The barrels are right behind us."

Penny had a mental picture of Lucille Ball stomping grapes, and didn't know if she wanted to see anyone's feet on what she drank. But like the good trooper she strived to be, she dutifully followed him after hanging up the last blouse she had brought.

So back through the hallways to the main staircase, but instead of out the front door, Kiley took left and steered her out past the kitchen and dining room down a narrow corridor and outside through a screen door.

The moonlight played peek-a-boo through the trees, the breeze warm on her skin. A gravel path led over a little hill where a gate hung invitingly. Kiley smiled down at her, grabbed her hand, and they walked toward it.

If Penny let fanciful notions into her head, she would imagine this a romantic evening, walking through the French countryside next to the most handsome man she had ever laid eyes on, having said man all to herself. The moon rose full and high in the sky, casting everything in a bluish tint, hiding any minor imperfections. Penny stole a glance behind her, at the so-called cottage, and saw it looked charming with almost every window lit up.

And the night was quiet, the type of quiet she hadn't had since leaving Missouri, where the only sound came from the crickets in unknown hiding spots and the rustle of moving wind through grass. It was one of those surreal moments in life, as if she and Kiley were the only two people left on earth, and she wished the moment didn't have to end.

But it did. As soon as they moved through the gate Penny saw an equally impressive home over the next hill, linked by the gravel road, surrounded by large wooden barns on one side and rows upon rows of grapes on the other.

She had seen a few grapevines, had taken a drive to northern California once, but Sonoma County had nothing on this. Even at night the sight was massive, the grapes hanging thick and red like sacks of blood. Several odd-shaped, tall machines rested in the rows, little wheels with tall legs straddling the vines, a picker designed not to crush the precious grapes.

As they walked, Kiley started pointing things out, telling stories of him and his cousins trying to steal the grapes, that turning into trying to steal the wine as they grew older. He was at home here, wearing jeans that hugged around his boxer shorts and a t-shirt, as he was in his leather pants and *haute couture* metrosexual sense, and she loved both sides to him equally.

She had to smile at that. She turned her head and watched him, allowing herself a few private minutes before they arrived at his uncle's house. She was glad she did when they became swarmed with a bevy of back-slapping family and barking dogs.

Kiley's family greeted and hugged her as if she were part of the family, and from the number of them, Penny figured she would be just another head to count. She met his uncle and aunt, their son, Jean-Jacques, his wife and their rather large family: five children, all boys, all hellions. Underfoot six dogs squealed and scampered. Penny almost felt afraid of moving in case she stepped on a tail or a foot.

It was hopeless trying to learn all their names, so she gave up. Kiley kept her by his side, whether if remembering the last time they were in a boisterous setting or just not wanting her to feel left out, she wasn't sure. But having his hand on her upper arm kept the smile upon her mouth all evening, even if she couldn't understand all that was being said. Every once in awhile the uncle or Jean-Jacques would speak a word or two in English, but it was clear they didn't speak that much, so Penny would smile and nod and let it all wash over her.

The young boys, ranging from ages from about ten to three, and obviously all flirts, had decided to impress Penny with giggling and poking her butt. While the parents sent them a stern word once or twice, it took Kiley grabbing hold of their fingers that put them to a stop. He bent down to swing the three-year-old up into his arms, ruffling the boy's blond curls and whispering in his ear. The little boy giggled and smashed his face into Kiley's neck before nodding. When Kiley set him down a second later, the little boy ran after his brothers and all the action soon moved away from the grownups.

About half an hour later, they moved from the house into the wine barns. Kiley's aunt stayed behind, washing up, and Jean-Jaques's wife went to try to put her little demons to bed. Just the four of them and a whole lot of wine, though Penny didn't know what to expect.

Inside the barn sat a dozen or so very large wooden barrels, blackened with age. A musty sour smell hung in the air, like spoiled vinegar and damp dirt, old, yet very sharp. It brought a smattering of tears to her eyes and she blinked several times to clear them.

"You'll get used to the smell," Kiley said to her. A long wooden table had bee pushed to one side with benches bracketing it and he directed her to sit. While the uncle and Jean-Jacques disappeared to gather some wine and some glasses, Kiley started to explain wine making to her. "The grapes are picked according to which type of wine is being made. For white wine the grapes are picked early in the season, and if it's red wine they're picked later, when they have ripened on the vine. They're dumped into that trough where they're skinned and pulped before heading into those vats to age. These vats have been in our family and in use for over a hundred years, which is why our wines are so delicious."

"What about stepping on the grapes, like in *I Love Lucy*?"

He laughed. "That's been replaced by technology I'm afraid."

At that moment Henri Macreaux returned and set several bottles of unlabeled wine in front of them. Jean-Jaques set three mismatched glasses down, a champagne flute, a brandy snifter and a proper wine glass, and a stein. Kiley immediately took the stein and his uncle laughed as he poured him a hefty amount in the goblet.

Penny got the wine glass, probably because she was the only woman, and had to admit the stuff tasted pretty good. The night wore on and the bottles became more and more empty. As the laughter and fun grew, Penny decided she liked this place and these people and most definitely, she loved Franc. The language barrier became a non-issue, because it was a pretty funny seeing her trying to teach the French winemakers how to speak English and they, in turn, trying to teach her French. Kiley kept laughing and kept refilling his stein, tears streaming from his eyes. He straddled the bench, facing her, with his uncle and cousin across from them, and he kept touching her. Even in her growing inebriated state, Penny noticed every touch and bump made her heart pound.

But she acted as if these little moments weren't precious to her, that they wouldn't forever be seared into her brain.

A little later, Jean-Jaques set another bottle in front of them with a snap. The bottle, once again unlabeled, was clear like water, and inside floated a dead snake.

"What the hell?" Penny muttered.

Kiley gave a groan as Jean-Jaques uncorked the bottle and took a swig before offering it to Henri. Henri took a swallow, passed it to Kiley who wanted to refuse, Penny could see the denial in his face, but couldn't when his uncle said something.

She watched in fascinated horror as he tipped the bottle back, took a deep drink, screwed up his face and gasped as the...whatever it was...burned to his stomach.

Then he handed it to her.

Penny looked at it before turning blank eyes at him. "What?" she asked stupidly.

He gave her a crooked smile. "Drink up."

She shook her head. "There's a dead snake in that."

"It's Snake Wine."

"That's what I said." She shook her head again.

Henri started teasing her and Jean-Jaques slapped her lightly on the back, talking to her in rapid French, and so, before she realized it, she had the bottle in her hand and took a drink.

It tasted like gasoline. It was potent, like drinking straight vodka, only vodka without flavor. Whatever this liquor was, it had been distilled far too long to get the highest proof possible with the absolute lack of taste. Her face crinkled up in disgust as she passed the bottle back to Jean-Jaques. Much to her horror, the damn thing came around again, the macabre snake a fascinating twist to the whole thing. Since the first swallow had burned out her taste buds, the second sip went down without problem.

"Waz 'da snake do?" she mumbled in broken grammar as she held the bottle again and brought it up to eye level. By this time, she had to squint to see clearly.

Kiley translated. Henri and Jean-Jaques laughed as Kiley explained. "Nothing really. Every time they catch a snake in the grapevines they make this stuff and keep him in there until it's gone."

"Mmm," she mumbled and took another drink.

At what time they decided to leave she hadn't a clue. After the second shot of Snake Wine everything pretty much became a haze. The next thing that stood out in her mind was her and Kiley stumbling home, with Kiley singing something way off-key and trying to teach her the words. They bumped into the gate and Penny thought it was extremely funny when they couldn't get it open, until Kiley remembered it swung the opposite way. The lights of the little "cottage" were still on, guiding them home, and Penny could vaguely recall where her bedroom was.

They helped each other up the stairs, laughing at impossible attempts to be silent, stumbling along the hallways until they came to her bedroom. Kiley helped take off her shoes, but as he tried to help her take off her jeans, they lost their balance and tipped backward onto the bed.

Oh what heaven to be in a bed, a very soft bed, with Kiley sprawled on top of her. Even in her drunken state of mind she loved every inch of him, the angles of his body hard where he needed to be hard, lush where he needed to be lush, fitting into her nicely. She wanted to hold him, squeeze him, kiss him, lick him....

That was her last thought before she passed out.

* * * *

It was around noon when she opened her eyes. Sunlight streamed in through the window. Birds chirruped loudly. A dog barked far in the distance. She wished she had a gun to shoot them all. Her head and vision swam as she looked around the room and down at herself.

She was half-dressed and alone, curled up under her comforter. She didn't want to move, but the way her stomach rolled around, she knew she would have to find a bathroom soon. She sat up and her vision went squirrelly. It was quite odd to see the room rolling around, as if she were on a ship and great waves were thrashing her back and forth.

The thought ended there as her stomach just revolted against such images, and she jumped out of bed and ran to her bathroom, barely making it as she threw open the toilet and emptied the contents she had remaining. Once the episode was over, she sat back on the cool tile and stayed there, nausea washing through her along with regret she had done something so foolish as to drink a substance with a snake floating in it.

That thought made her reach for the toilet again, and once her second round finished, she rather thought she was feeling better. Her stomach had stopped rumbling and her eyes had stopped swimming around. She still felt wretched, however, and decided going back to bed was just the thing. But as she stood and leaned for a moment against the wall, she felt someone staring at her.

Kiley stood in the doorway, looking pale and tired. His hair was pulled back in a little pony tail and he had loose swimming trunks knotted around his hips.

She grunted a greeting to him and reached for her toothbrush.

"I had that a little earlier," he grunted back, nodding to the toilet.

She brushed her teeth and washed her face. The cold water helped settle her a little more.

"Put your bathing suit on," he ordered, turning as she moved past him.

"I don't feel like swimming."

"Neither do I," he replied. "But the sun and warmth will do wonders."

Though she doubted this highly, she shooed him out, changed, and met him by the pool. He lay on a lounge chair, sunglasses in place, a bottle of sunscreen next to him. She pulled her own chair into the shade, laid down, and fell asleep.

* * * *

She woke up when she heard a splash and lifted her head to see Kiley swimming laps in the pool. How long she had slept she didn't know but it was clearly on the end scale of day, near evening with twilight approaching.

"Come on in," he told her with a wave. "It's warm."

"Nah," she murmured, closing her eyes again. "Can't swim with the stitches."

She heard him pull himself from the pool and flinched as several cool drops of water hit her. She cracked an eye and looked at him.

"Are you hungry?"

She thought about it. "Yeah. I am."

He turned and walked back to his lounger, grabbing his towel and rubbing himself off. "Give me about half an hour."

"You're going to cook?

He slung the towel over his back and gave her a funny grin. "No, *Madame* Mourre is, but I'll join you in the dining room in half an hour."

He winked and walked away. Like a cat eyeing a mouse, she watched him walk away, deciding that the low riding trunks looked just as sexy as those black leather pants he always wore.

Chapter 20

Penny wasn't feeling back to her normal self until the next day. The nagging headache had disappeared with a decent night sleep and, as she rose the next morning, energy bounced through her.

She showered, threw on a pair of khaki shorts and a nice cotton blouse, brushed her hair back and decided to let it hang free. She left her room to find Kiley. His door was closed so she knocked once.

A second later he yanked open and Kiley stood there with a towel around his hips, a toothbrush in his mouth, and nothing else. She couldn't help it—really, what woman could? She looked him up and down. She met his one-raised-eyebrow-mocking stare and had to take a step back.

"Well," she cleared her throat, "I see you're still getting ready." She pointed over her shoulder. "I'll see you at breakfast."

She turned and fled down the hallway, his amused laugh floating behind her.

* * * *

"Do you like bikes?" he asked as he sat next to her at the table.

Penny took a sip of coffee to wash down the last of her food. "I know how to ride one, why?"

"We're going on a picnic."

"And we need bikes for that?"

He nodded, slathering a piece of toast with strawberry jam.

"And you have bikes for both of us?"

He nodded again, taking a large bite of his toast.

Penny narrowed her eyes. "I haven't actually ridden a bike in about ten years. Am I going to have a sore ass when we finally get to our picnic?"

He had been taking a sip of coffee when she asked, and he gave a strangled gurgle as he half laughed in the liquid. He calmly sat his cup down and gave her a lascivious wink. "If it is, I'll gladly rub it to make it feel better."

Heat stole over her cheeks, but she held his gaze. There was something different about Kiley lately. He was relaxed, calm, and all his attention seemed to be on her.

"What's going on behind those blue eyes of yours?" she asked him.

He gave her a wink, rose and held out his hand to help her up. "Why don't you get the basket *Madame* Mourre has done up for us and meet me out back by the shed."

She watched him walk away, her heart racing, knowing he planned something. She could feel it and wondered what it could be. So she took a few extra minutes to grab her sunglasses and sunscreen before she gathered the basket, smiling shyly at *Madame* Mourre, and headed out to see two bikes side by side and Kiley talking with *Monsieur* Mourre. His, she noticed, was a ten-speed racing bike, while hers had a nice little wire basket on the front.

She placed the picnic basket in the wire one. "Trying to tell me something?" she asked with a gesture to the granny bike.

Kiley laughed. "Just trying to spare your ass."

Hi wave at *Monsieur* Mourre spared her from answering. He rolled his bike forward to straddle it. "Ready?" he asked, looking over his shoulder at her.

She shrugged and mounted hers. "Lead on, O fearless leader."

And off they went. Though she had seen much of the countryside, this gave her a whole different experience from an open view. Smells came to her: the scent of flowers, the slight sourness from the grapevines, the clean air itself. She heard the buzz of bees and felt the whip of wind as they rode through the town and out along the narrow lane toward several open fields. The land rolled and dipped and several times she could make out stone houses in the patches of grapevines and cultivated farmland. The sun shone, warming her skin, feeling like pure heaven. Surely no place on earth could be as beautiful or peaceful in that particular moment in time, and it was a surreal moment forever branded in her memory.

She watched Kiley as he led the way, admiring how his white knee-length cutoffs hugged his backside as he peddled, how his sandals showed off trim calves, how his white muscle shirt accentuated his muscular arms. He wore a white fishing hat over his hair and dark sunglasses.

They rode for over twenty minutes on the road, mindful of cars that passed them, before Kiley turned onto a compact dirt path. It seemed to be a park of some kind, with various nature signs and several picnic tables. They passed it all and emerged from the shadowed path into an open field, and much to her dismay, a hill.

She fell behind him as she made her way up, feeling the burn through her legs and butt as she continued to peddle. But she kept at it and eventually reached the top, seeing Kiley dismounted from his bike and kickstanded it to one side. He waited for her before grabbing the picnic basket as she came to a panting stop next to him.

He led her into a field, up another hill, until it leveled out in a sea of flowers overlooking the entire valley they had just ridden through. There were no trees to offer shade, but she didn't care, as Kiley pulled out a blanket from the basket and spread it out on the ground. In this small paradise they were alone, just them and flowers and the occasional bee.

"This is amazing," she murmured looking out over the countryside.

"It's one of my favorite places in the world," he told her, uncorking a bottle of red wine. He poured her a glass and handed it to her. She sat down and took it, clinking it with his as he held his own out to a toast.

"What shall we drink to?"

"The Lakers winning the playoffs."

She laughed. "You don't watch basketball."

"I do when the Lakers are winning. Hmm...all right, to Papillon."

"To Papillon."

"Let's see what *Madame* Mourre made for us," he murmured and started pulling out sandwiches, strawberries, a tin of caviar, salad, olives stuffed with anchovies, fried chicken, and four different kinds of cheese. Plates and utensils were located at the bottom along with another bottle of wine.

"Wow," Penny said, eyeing the goodies.

Kiley removed his sunglasses and took off his sandals after he had made himself a plate, propping himself on one elbow and lying on one hip. He ate and watched her.

"What?" she asked after swallowing a bite of ham sandwich.

"Why did you stay in the shadows at the party Luci held?"

She shrugged. "I didn't know anyone there really, except for you and Antoinette and Lucien."

"I kept looking for you to introduce you."

She raised an eyebrow. "You didn't need to introduce your secretary."

He shook his head. "We don't use the 'S' word, remember? In any case, not as my employee, but as my partner."

The bite she had just taken turned to dust in her mouth and she had to take a swallow of wine to wash it down. "What?" she squeaked.

"I want you to be my partner at Papillon," he clarified.

She looked at him, searching for signs of a fever...dementia...anything to explain what he just said. "I'm...."

That was as far as she got. Speechlessness took over.

"You're dedicated to the gallery, you work just as hard as I do, you're wonderful with clients. You know art." He shrugged with his free shoulder. "We're alike, you and I, and I know we'd make compatible partners."

"Kiley...I don't know what to say." Tears sprung in her eyes and she sat her sandwich aside.

"Hey," he sat up. "I didn't mean to make you cry."

She shook her head. "I'm happy and overwhelmed. Shocked. Giddy." She took her sunglasses off to stare into his bare eyes. "You trust me that much?" she whispered.

He reached out and cupped her chin. "I trust you that much."

She wanted him to kiss her, yearned for him to lean down the last few inches. Her eyes darted his lips and watched them, licking her own in preparation for his mouth on hers.

But the moment shattered as he pulled back, turning away to pick his sandwich back up and taking a hefty drink of his wine, leaving Penny to blink at the sudden loss.

"When we get back home, to Los Angeles, I'll have the paperwork drawn up," he murmured, as if the pull between them hadn't existed.

"I can't really afford to buy into the gallery, Kiley," she muttered as she reined in her thoughts, refilling her glass.

He waved the words away. "Don't worry about it now. We'll concentrate on all that when we get home. I just want you to know that I want you permanently in Papillon's life."

What about yours? she wanted to ask. Sadly, she didn't have the guts to ask him aloud.

* * * *

The phone picked up on the third ring. "Hello?" came Lark's disgruntled voice. Penny winced, knowing it was probably way too early to be calling California.

"Lark?"

A heartbeat, then, "Penny? Aren't you in France?"

"Yes."

"How are you calling me?"

"They do have telephones here, silly."

"That's not what I meant, Miss Smarty Pants."

"I'm calling from the family chateau of Kiley Laurent, somewhere in the middle of France, complete with suit of armor, family crest, and two servants."

"Cool," Lark breathed, clearly impressed. "And since you mentioned Mister GQ, how is the lovely boss man?"

"Lovely," Penny replied.

"Is that a bit of dreamy quality I hear ringing in your voice through the confusing world of wireless phones?"

"I'm not wireless, and yes...dreamy. This trip has been a revelation, Lark. Well, except for the snake wine."

"The what?"

"Long story. Long hangover."

"That sounds so gross."

"Wait till I tell you about the unisex bathroom." Penny giggled.

"Can't wait," Lark said in a tone that belied the statement.

"Guess what."

"You're engaged?"

"Um, no. But good fantasy there, Lark. No, Kiley asked me to be his partner!"

"I thought you said you're not engaged."

"No, no. Art partner! He wants me to be his partner at Papillon!"

"Oh, Penny, that is wonderful. I'm so happy for you! When you get back we'll go out and celebrate."

"It's a date!"

"How are you doing, besides that? How are those stitches?"

"Still in. Itching a lot. It's hard keeping them dry, especially since there's a pool out front. Really, Lark, you would love this countryside."

"Ahem," Lark coughed. "I am not a country girl, remember? If there isn't a happening club and a handy man nearby I ain't going."

Penny laughed. "I miss you, Lark."

"Right back at ya. Hey, bring me back a souvenir."

"What would you like?"

"Anything, but if it has a snake in it, I'm going to bop you over the head."

* * * *

That evening another of Kiley's cousins showed up and Lark's words came back to haunt Penny. Marie was a female version of Kiley, laughing as she bounded up to him to give him a tight hug, talking a mile a minute.

Kiley laughed and calmed her down long enough to introduce her. "Marie," he said in English, "this is Penny Varlet. Penny, my ditzy cousin, Marie Sirmain, who lives in town."

Marie punched his arm. "*Oui*, I had to hear you were visiting from Gerald, who heard from Phillipe, who found out from Jean-Jacques." She placed dainty fists on her dainty hips and glared at her cousin for a moment. "There are no more pastries at Gerald's, by the way," she added before she turned and graced a warm smile on Penny. "It is very nice to meet you, Penny," she said in a lightly accented fashion. She leaned over and kissed first one cheek and than the other in typical European greeting. "I have come to gather you both for The Cave."

Kiley groaned. "No, we're both still recovering from Uncle Henri's Snake Wine."

Penny gave a little shudder at that mention which Marie noticed and laughed. "My husband has that same reaction every time I mention father's secret weapon."

"What is The Cave?" Penny asked cautiously, deciding to best get off the subject of that horrid drink.

"There is a noise restriction here," Kiley explained, "which used to cause the teenage population to go insane."

"So we built an underground club," Marie finished, grinning, "and called it The Cave. It is very hip-hop." She gave an "O-K" sign with her fingers.

"We don't have to go—" Kiley started off.

"I'd love to go," Penny interrupted.

Marie slapped her hands together and grabbed Penny's hands. "Come, take me to your room. Let us get you made up!"

Penny glanced once over her shoulder to throw a helpless look toward Kiley as Marie dragged her off up the stairs, but Kiley only gave her a shrug as if saying "You wanted to go."

And in her bedroom Marie was like a tornado. "The Cave draws people from all over so we must make you *appetissant*."

"Make me what?"

Marie held up her black dress before throwing it aside. Penny looked at it ruefully. That had been what she had been going to wear. Old Faithful.

"Um...appetizing." By now her entire suitcase had been emptied and Marie looked around the clothes scattered around the bed, hands on her hips. Though she should be frowning at the mess and her presumptuous nature, Penny had never met a woman like her before.

"You must come home with me," Marie said, turning to face her.

"Why?"

"I've something for you to wear."

"Something appetizing?"

"*Oui*!" She grabbed Penny's hand and marched her out the door, pausing long enough to knock once on Kiley's door before poking her head in. Penny heard a yelp from Kiley inside. "Like I haven't seen that before," Marie replied in dry tone. She looked quickly back at Penny, who stood to one side in the hallway, and rolled her eyes. "He and I grew up together since little babies. Our *mamans* used to bathe us together. Really, he's gotten quite shy from American influence."

With that she yelled something out in French, grabbed Penny's hand again, and they quickly left.

* * * *

Marie's house wasn't quite as large as the chateau but it was fairly impressive in its own right...like a large farmhouse nestled in the woods. Marie introduced Penny to her husband, Christophe, who smiled absently from over several open journals, before shuffling her upstairs into her bedroom.

"Don't mind him," Marie said with a smile. "He is studying."

"He's a student?"

"No. He studies soil for my *pere*. For the wine."

Penny nodded as if she understood, when in fact, she didn't. But that was neither here nor there as she faced a bigger problem. Or rather, a smaller problem. "Marie...I can't fit into your clothes. You're about a size smaller than me."

What was it with the French? They were all tiny but lived on wine, cheese and rich creamy sauces.

Marie eyed her. "No, you are just taller. Try these on...."

Half an hour later, Penny stood in front of The Cave entrance next to a working barn. A set of stone steps lead down into the ground to a thick door, which was surprisingly heavy. A corridor opened up which lead to another door. Penny could hear music thumping heavy.

"Oh, I love this song!" Marie squealed.

Penny wore a pair of tight, white Alvin Valley sailor Capri pants that had three large buttons on each side. Marie put her in tight little tank, black, that narrowed her hips and accentuated her bust. Marie had also fluffed her hair up and used several small clips to make it look messy in a controlled way. She also had applied more makeup than she had ever worn before, dark eyeliner that brought out her dark eyes, and several coats of mascara.

Penny wasn't sure why Marie had dressed them both up so much until she pushed open the second door and saw what The Cave was actually about. A bar stood at one end, two waiters serving drinks, running back and forth in the demand of the line. Several tables were present, filled with bodies huddled around. Through an archway she saw a light show and bodies dancing through the flashing lights. Music throbbed through the air, hitting her body and making her want to go out and join them. It was infectious.

Marie grabbed her hand and wove their way through the throngs of people, finding it hard to believe there were that many people in the area around their age. The Cave was filled, some of them questionable about legal age.

Several men and women greeted Marie, though it was too loud to make conversation. A wave, a smile or kissed cheeks were all they got, and Penny was greeted the same way though she didn't know any of them. The song changed, one sliding into another, as she found herself on the crowded dance floor.

She danced to the electric rhythm and her hips moved, her body swayed, with her arms out in front of her. Partners around her who gyrated to the beat as well flashed in and out of her dance sight, moving with her for a few moments and then moving on. She lost herself. She felt different, almost wicked as she closed her eyes and swayed to the beat. And when hands grab her hips, bringing her ass close into a very male pelvis, she knew it was Kiley who conquered her. His palms burned where they held her, the heat of his chest branded her back. Her body moved with his, sliding side to side, seducing. She grabbed the back of his neck, linking them closer as he bent his head near her own. They moved as one, fluid, the rest of the dancers fading.

How long they danced she didn't know, and it was magic. He slid his fingers along her jaw as he kissed her, right there on the dance floor and amid the strobe lights. He was hard for her, hard and wanting, while his tongue invaded and claimed her own. Penny wanted it, craved it, craved him with a desire that made her thrust her rear into his pelvis, as if she were a bitch in heat.

Seconds later, her hand firmly planted in his, they wove their way through the crowd. He half dragged her out of The Cave, and only when the moonlight hit did she notice he wore his black leather pants. Black leather and a black fishnet muscle shirt. They move into the shadows of the barn, becoming part of the darkness with only small moans a telltale sign that they were there.

His lips nibbled on the outer edges of her mouth, taking feather licks with his tongue. His right hand came up to cup her chin, his thumb moved up rub where their mouths fused, seeking, searching and so incredibly hot. This touch left flames dancing over her skin. She opened her mouth to suck in the heat and that was the answer he sought. Her moan drowned in the wave of his onslaught as he swept in to explore her, taste her, fill her. His other hand moved down her back, slowly as if an afterthought, until it rested where her hips flared out. He pulled her closer to him, fitting her in the curve of his body. To his hard planes and angles, she molded lush and soft. Her breasts pushed against his chest and deep in his throat he gave a guttural groan.

He wrenched his mouth from hers causing the ache inside to burst out in a moan and she opened her eyes to meet his hungry blue gaze. She shivered, sure the fire between them would burn her alive.

"I want you," he whispered, almost achingly.

"Then take me," she whispered back.

His fingers made their way into her capris, but instead of reaching for her slick walls, his fingers tread their way to her ass, a hand cupping each cheek to pull her more firmly into the arch of his groin. With a wiggle, she begged for more.

His fingers eased under the fragile scrap of material that disappeared between her cheeks, skimming lightly over her puckered hole before quickly moving to give her slit a caress. Her belly tightened in either anticipation or trepidation. She wasn't quite sure which one was the more dominant feeling.

A second later, his hands left her pants as he flipped her around and placed her hands up high against the wooden wall of the barn, his breath hot against her neck. He leaned closer and took a nip from her shoulder, licking the skin to sooth it. He repeated the love bite directly over her spine at the base of her neck, her skin highly sensitive. She gasped and arched in pleasure.

He pulled her hips out a little more toward him as he pushed her head over more, making her ass stick out. Her pants were pushed to her knees. The posture parted her ass cheeks, and she felt Kiley repeat his earlier caress, pushing her thong aside to brush lightly over her puckered anus. He ran his fingers through her pussy juice, coating them to continue his exploration of her anus, pushing the tip of one finger in and causing her to hiss.

"Kiley!" she breathed half in fear, half in curiosity.

"Shh," he whispered as he pushed his finger in a little more.

She heard his zipper. With one finger up her ass, he pushed his cock into her cunt, filling her as she had never been filled before. His free hand reached around to grab her breast, teasing the nipple into a hard pebble. A sheen broke out onto her face as he started to see-saw his way in and out of her, the finger finding the same rhythm to send her senses into overdrive.

"Tell me you love me fucking you like this," he demanded, a quiver betraying how he was also affected.

"Yes," she moaned back, "yes, yes…oh!"

He grunted loudly as his cock started to twitch out of control. Both withered against the first tingle of orgasm as it swept them both up. He pounded her, and she could feel it coming, his and hers. Together they embraced it, the flush of heat as he gripped her hips tightly and thrust so deeply, she wasn't sure where he ended and she began. Jet after jet filled her, triggering her own orgasm as she felt it coat her insides, until his spasming body relaxed from its pleasure plateau.

He panted heavy against her hair, his heart thundering like a racehorse after winning the Derby. He withdrew his finger from her ass and let his deflating cock slip from her still quivering pussy. Cum immediately started to trickle down her thigh, but she just pulled her pants up and hoped it didn't stain the pants.

Kiley tucked himself back in, grabbed her hand with a satisfied smile, and made his way toward the car.

He sped back to the chateau and neither one of them spoke, though he popped in a disc and the music blared inside the car, filling up her head again and making her sway in the seat.

When they got home, Kiley shut off the motor and they exited the car. Penny waited for Kiley to come to her and escort her in. She looked up at the chateau, lit, waiting for their return.

He took hold of her hand and they looked at one another, almost shyly. She smiled and her eyes fell to his lips as he bent and captured hers, the kiss tender and sweet. It took her breath away. He took his time, made it gentle. Her mouth moved under his but she followed his lead, letting the moment build as the anticipation grew. In that kiss they learned a thousand things about each other in an instant: the way their breaths moved in and out and fitted each others perfectly, the way their hearts quickened at the merest hint of friction, the way each other smelt and felt as noses nudged and lips teased.

She was lost. Floating. There were stars behind her lids and everything ceased to exist except the exquisite torture he nursed on her mouth and the hardness between her thighs she salivated for. She was helpless, a puppet dangling on the strings he pulled, but she craved it all. He swept her up in his arms and carried her up the stairs to his room.

Chapter 21

The next morning's sky didn't quite match the lovely vision Penny had pictured after such a wonderful night. Gray with thick clouds hung like giant black puffs, no birds chirped, no sunshine warmed her, in fact she shivered and pulled the silky softness of Kiley's sheets closer to her chin. The double windows stood wide open and she threw it a baleful glare.

Except for being chilly, she felt wonderful, alive, and accepted, not like the other two times when she had felt confused and mortified after sex with Kiley. Somehow, this time, they had just been two people, not boss and employee, meeting and loving. Last night had definitely been about making love and she let the feeling wash over her.

A perfect morning, even with the thunderclouds.

She heard no running water, or sounds from the adjoining bathroom to indicate he was in there, so she sat up holding the sheet to her chest. Hoping Kiley would get her ESP vibe to come back and join her in bed, she waited for five minutes before realizing the mental summons wasn't going to work. So she stood and reached for her borrowed clothes, hurrying into them to fend off the cold air, and made her way to her own room to wash up in record time.

With wet hair brushed neatly back, Penny folded Marie's clothes and set them aside, looked at her own collection of clothes and had to laugh at herself for dragging so much with her.

"Hey you," Kiley's rich voice said from the doorway.

Penny turned, still smiling. "Hey, right back at you."

He walked into the room and took her in his arms. "What are you smiling about?"

"Myself for bringing this hefty suitcase with me, when we were just staying a few days."

Kiley shrugged. "I have no plans to rush back to Paris."

His eyes were dark with arousal. She shifted her hips closer and felt the evidence through the sweatpants she had put on while she finished her toilette. He leaned over her and groaned, his breath ruffling a few strips of hair over her ears.

"I came up here to get you. *Madame* Mourre has breakfast fixed, waiting for us."

"Mmm," she murmured back into his chest, her fingers running up and down his back. "What if we're late?"

"She'll come up here to find us," he muttered, regretfully.

Penny pulled back. "We can't be too tardy, is that what you're saying?"

She started backing up to the bed, pulling him with her.

Kiley eyed their destination. "We only have ten minutes, tops, before she comes looking for us."

A wicked smile graced her lips. "Well, we better be fast. Fast and hard."

Her wicked smile caused him to close the door.

* * * *

Twenty minutes later they both made their way down the stairs toward the dining room where Madame Mourre waited, hands on hips, but with a twinkle in her dark eyes. Penny blushed and looked at the floor as Madame Mourre said something to Kiley and shook her finger at him before retreating out of the room. On the table several dishes of delicious smelling food tempted and beckoned.

"What did she say?"

Kiley shook his head. "You don't want to know."

With the weather so bad outside, they didn't rush through the meal. She felt at peace as they sat at the large table in the large room, close enough to Kiley that it felt cozy. They talked about various topics, subjects, whatever happened to pop into their minds, the after-dinner coffee hot and delicious on just such a day.

Long after their bellies were sated, they moved from the dining room to what could only be the family room. Surprisingly only a radio sat on the mantel, no television in sight.

"My parents didn't want us watching TV when we were here," Kiley explained when she questioned him. "But we have lots and lots of games."

They spent the rest of the day playing board games like Monopoly, Clue, and Scrabble, though the last one very odd to play since the pieces were in the French language, giving her more 'z's to use up.. In the evening they picked up a deck of cards and decided to play poker, using cookies Madame Mourre had baked earlier in the day as the chips.

"I win again," Penny announced as she laid down her four aces, beating his full house. "Do you have any cigars? I feel like twirling a cigar at my winnings."

Kiley reached over, picked up one of her cookies, and ate it in one bite.

"Hey!" She laughed, bopping him on the head with a couch pillow.

This led to his swift retaliation. He pounced on her, tickling her and making her squeal and start a counterattack. Back and forth they went, stalking, pouncing, and playing. Penny couldn't remember when she had had more fun, or when she had seen Kiley laugh so hard.

"I have an idea," she mused.

"What's that?"

She licked her lips. "Why don't we change this to strip poker? And with my wins I say take off everything from the waist down."

Kiley stood and proceeded to very slowly hook his thumbs under the elastic band of his shorts and tug them down a fraction. "Are you sure you want this?"

Her eyes caught his until his hips swished, bringing the shorts down a little bit more. Her eyes took a dive south.

Skin, tight and toned, met her eyes. The flat plane of his stomach gave way to the baby fine hairs. He was aroused by her perusal. There was no hiding it when the tip peaked through the top. Penny licked her lips, her mouth watering to swallow him deep.

The shorts came down a little bit more, exposing more to her hungry eyes and salivating palate. He took a step forward, bringing her into direct eye contact with his stiff cock, a bead of moisture appearing to break her control.

She leaned forward and flicked her tongue just under the head's rim, and smiled as his cock jumped from the slight contact. Her tongue captured the dew drops weeping from the slit, causing him to groan in mounting excitement. Even as she started to engulf him with her mouth, her tongue kept flicking back to the opening to milk him.

She shuffled forward and ran her tongue around him, licking him clean, until she heard his moan and felt his knees shake. She grabbed a butt cheek in each hand, her fingernails digging into the firm flesh as she slid her lips over him.

Her tongue traced every vein bulging from her oral play. Kiley placed his hands on her head, keeping her mouth on him. She started out slowly, up and down, creating a suction that had him panting with need. One hand moved around and wrapped it around the base on his penis while her other hand came around to play with his balls. As she moved back down the shaft, she engulfed him all the way until the tip hit the back of her throat and gave swallowing motions to caress it a different way.

He let out a guttural sound and she released him, lifting the shaft to suck one testicle into her mouth. She rolled it around, sucking, before taking the other in her mouth and duplicating the nibble. He pressed against her head and she took his cock back into her mouth, plunging him deep and speeding up the tempo. The entire time her tongue flickered around his cock like a velvet glove.

His fingers buried in her hair, holding her still. "I'm on the verge," he growled, panting.

She tipped her head back. "I know," she whispered in a husky, sexy voice. She returned to her treat, feeling him swell and grow even harder. Penny opened her eyes, catching his feral gaze, and felt cum blast the back of her throat. Quickly, greedily, she swallowed, some leaking out of her mouth to dribble down her chin.

With the last spurt, Kiley slumped over her, his hands releasing the death grip on her hair. Penny listened to his heart racing, giddy with the thought she brought him so much pleasure.

Later that night, they lay side by side.

"Thank you for coming here with me."

She turned his gaze and met his tenderly. "This has been amazing. I can't imagine growing up with this as a summer home."

"Did you have a summer vacation place?"

She smiled. "My parents had a mobile home, and a spot reserved at Current River. We'd go every summer for a couple of weeks. I would inner-tube down the river and swim every morning, though it'd be freezing. And my dad would go gigging and fishing with other men, so we'd have this huge fish fry."

"I don't know half of what you said, but it sounds like you were a happy kid."

She nodded. "It was some of the best times of my childhood."

"But it was too small for you," he concluded.

"Yeah."

"Paris was too big for me."

She studied his face, trying to see past the man to the little boy he once had been. "It must have been hard being the child of parents whose legend had been established long before you."

He shrugged. "They were good parents." He turned his head back so he once again stared at the ceiling. "Except for the damn television."

* * * *

Sometime in the night she heard a phone ringing, but it didn't register too highly in her mind. Her body noticed Kiley went missing and it turned to where his warmth still lingered. She drifted in limbo until she felt a gentle hand shaking her.

"Penny, sweetheart, wake up," Kiley's voice insisted.

"Mmm," she moaned and tried to bury deeper into the blankets.

"Penny," Kiley said more firmly.

She squinted one eye open to him. "What?" she mumbled. There was such a sad, despondent look on his face that all sleep disappeared and she sat up in panic. "Kiley?"

"That was Detective Proper."

The sadness in his eyes scared her. "What happened, Kiley?"

"It's Jed," he finally sighed and ran a hand through his already mused hair. "He committed suicide, Penny. We need to go back to Los Angeles."

* * * *

They headed back to Paris that night after packing quickly and rousing a sleepy-eyed Monsieur Mourre to explain what had happened. Penny left Marie's clothes for her in the front foyer, next to a particularly dour looking Laurent ancestor, with a quick note of thanks.

They hardly spoke on the drive back, each lost in depressing memories of Jed. Detective Proper hadn't gone into details, only asked if they would consider returning to Los Angeles as quickly as they could.

They drove into Paris by afternoon and made straight for his parents' home. With all her stuff packed, Kiley made reservations for the first flight out and his father took them right over to the airport. Penny gave tight hugs to Lilyane and Alain Laurent, as Kiley retrieved her suitcase. He hadn't bothered to pack any of his stuff, asking his mother to send it to him instead. He shook his father's hand, kissed his mother good-bye and waved one last time as they disappeared inside the airport.

Chapter 22

Penny stood in her austere black dress, a frown tugging on her lips as she sat at Jedidiah Yuki's funeral and listened to the minister give a sermon for a man he obviously didn't know. The eulogy was nothing more than a generic stale reading from the Bible.

Things had happened quickly and somberly as she and Kiley returned to Los Angeles and made their way to the police station to talk to Detective Proper. He had handed them a note, the suicide note from Jed, which apologized in an agonizing tone and told them the only restitution he could give his name and his art was immortality. He had asked Kiley to keep his paintings safe, and when the right time presented itself, put on the show that had always meant to happen. It was a bitter last request. They hadn't asked for details on how Jed had died. They frankly didn't care. Kiley had handed the note back to the Detective without a word.

They talked to the lawyer Jed had hired, finding out that all Jed's work had been left to Papillon Gallery, so even if Kiley wanted to decline his last request, the art would still be there.

A distant family member had shown up to take care of the memorial service and the burial plans, much to Penny's relief. So she sat there without Kiley, who had refused to attend, listening to a minister recite some bland scripture about the kingdom of heaven and eternal forgiveness, when all she wanted to do was get up and leave. Only a handful of people had shown up so she forced herself to remain seated until the reading finished and the eulogy came to a close. She sighed, rose, and made her way out of the stale smelling room that had been overly scented with cloying sweet odor of lilies and carnations. Once outside she took a deep breath of the Los Angeles air, enjoying the rush of motor fumes and salty tang that rushed into her lungs.

The funeral parlor's doors opened and several people filed out, people she recognized who had sat through Jed's service. They didn't stop to talk to her, only bowed their heads as they made their way to their various means of transportation. That's when her eyes fell on Lark.

"What are you doing here?" she asked as she finished walking the few steps down to meet her friend.

Lark gave her a small, supportive smile. "Thought I'd see how you were doing." She looked around the quiet street, her eyes lingering for a moment on the people walking away from the funeral homes to their cars. "Want to go for a walk?"

Penny nodded.

They walked for a minute in silence, whether because of the circumstances she had just left or not Penny didn't know, but she appreciated the gesture. It gave her a moment to collect herself.

"You took a day off work for me?" she finally asked.

"It's Monday. Nothing really important happens on a Monday," Lark replied with a shrug. "The demanding jerk for a director will just have to tough it out for a day."

"Oh, is he back for another episode?"

"The powers that be must have overlooked my veto bill. Oh well, I guess I'll find out what really makes him so pushy this evening."

Penny squinted an eye at her. "And what is happening this evening?"

"My date with him."

"I thought you didn't like him."

"I don't." Lark shrugged then brought her hands to her chest and started measuring with them. "But he has pecs out to here that I really can't ignore. What's a girl to do?"

Penny rolled her eyes and smiled.

"Ah ha!" Lark cried with a pointed finger. "Finally! You crack a smile and it only took me," she looked at her watch, "five minutes thirty-three seconds."

Penny sighed. "Sorry. It's just...so much has happened in the past month. My head is all in a jumble."

"Mmm, I can imagine. That is why we are heading to Melrose right now."

"Excuse me?"

"Time to turn your frown upside down."

Penny stopped dead in her tracks. It took a few steps for Lark to realize her friend no longer walked beside her. "Penny?"

"I just came from a funeral, Lark. How can you possibly think about shopping?"

"I always think about shopping, my dear."

Penny came to a halt. "A man took his life—"

"And you're not responsible," Lark interrupted firmly. She took Penny's hand. "I know what you're thinking. I know you. You are *not* responsible for Jed's death."

Penny gave a huff. "What a silly thing to say. I know that I was in France."

Lark shook her head. "I was speaking metaphorically. Penny, the man had no sense to the value of his life. His work was brilliant but no one will remember him for that. They will barely remember his name."

"Don't you think I realize that?" Her brows creased together. "He took his life for what he did to me."

"No. He took his life because he couldn't accept the consequences of his actions." Lark shook her head. "It was his choices, his decisions. And you have no reason to feel guilty."

Penny opened and closed her mouth in one breath. "All right. You do know me."

"So that's why we are going to Melrose."

"To shop."

"To change."

"Come again?"

Lark placed her hands on Penny's shoulders. "For a while I've seen you struggling. With yourself, with your place in Kiley's life, and with how you feel in your own skin. It's time, my dear, for a change. It's time for affirmative action."

"Oh really?"

Lark nodded. "Really. And in taking those actions you will melt away all the doubts and fears your little country heart has."

The last lesson in life, Penny supposed, remembering the break-in and the knife and thinking how close she, herself, had come to being buried with lilies and carnations. Yet here she stood, and a million miles from the Penny Varlet that had lived through that time.

Lark's cell phone rang, interrupting her thoughts.

"Here, it's for you. It's Kiley."

"Why is Kiley calling your phone?"

"Because, you nitwit, you don't have one."

"Oh, right." She put the phone to her ear. "Hello?"

"What are your plans for this evening?"

"Um...nothing planned."

"Meet me at the Gallery."

"Is this an order?"

He paused for a moment. "Please."

"Since you asked so nicely," she murmured. "I'll see you later."

"Thank you, Penny." He rang off.

She was left holding the phone, wondering about his rather abrupt tone.

* * * *

The trip on Melrose Avenue became a liberating point to Penny. She felt free and that influenced her shopping, gravitating toward a different sense of self. Gone was the desire to hide in her faded jeans, oversized dresses, unflattering tops and blouses. She had defied her credit card company by almost maxing it out with her new wardrobe.

Penny carried all her new goodies into her bedroom and proceeded to toss out all her old and unflattering garments. She moved into her bathroom and added to the discard pile all her headbands. They had serviced the old Penny wonderfully, but that wasn't who she was anymore.

She turned on her radio, which had still been tuned to the station Kiley had it on the last time he had been over. She stood there for a moment, hands on her hips, as she listened to the music for a moment. With a distasteful grimace, she flicked it off and moved to her CD player. A moment later the very peaceful sound of Enya came through the speakers. Okay, things were meant to be different, but not over the top. Penny hummed along as she snipped price tags and hung up outfits, happy with her choices. She changed into an outfit similar to what Marie had let her borrow and placed the black funeral dress on the pile of stuff to take to Goodwill. She stood back and stared at her closet.

She wiped her hands together, as if brushing dust off. She had a lot more room now that it wasn't crammed with old and faded clothes, too tight clothes, too big clothes, or clothes that her grandmother had sent her. Slipping on some new clogs, she shut the closet door and turned to heave the pile of discarded stuff out the door.

"Hello, dear," Mrs. Shackelton said as the elevator doors opened.

"Hello, Mrs. Shackelton," Penny replied as she pulled the box inside and hit the ground floor level.

"How are you doing? Didn't have a relapse did you?"

Penny shook her head. "No, I went on vacation."

"Oh good, good. I hope with that handsome blond fellow of yours." She raised her pencil drawn eyebrows up. "What a hot dish."

"Mrs. Shackelton!" Penny gasped in a teasing voice.

The elderly woman waved her hand. "Go on. Off with you, dearie. Back in my day I had many a nice vacation with handsome blond men. I highly recommend it."

Penny continued to chuckle as the elevator doors opened.

Mrs. Shackelton gave her a wink as they parted at the front door. "Hope you have many more nice vacations. If not, send him up to my apartment."

Penny drove to the nearest Goodwill, and the workers were all smiles as they accepted her offering. After stashing the receipt in her glove box, along with various other pieces of supposedly important papers, and making a mental bet she'd never see the receipt again, she set off once more, heading to Papillon.

The Gallery waited for her, like an old friend, and Penny had to take a deep breath as she realized this would be the first time she would walk into the building after almost dying in it. It looked different, somehow. Brighter. Bigger. It took her a few minutes to realize there yellow gerberas and button spray chrysanthemums had been planted in front of the massive glass walls, in a new, very green, manicured lawn. She liked it, she decided, as she made her way up the entry steps.

The door stood open.

"Hello?" she called out.

Something felt different about the place, a different atmosphere, and wasn't sure if it was the dark memory of the past or a new paint job that gave the effect. She looked up to see tape around the beveled glass of the window that overlooked into the gallery from Kiley's office.

"That's how they got you," Kiley's smooth voice said, causing her to jump and place a hand to her heart as she turned to face him.

She saw his gaze run up and down her body, noting the new clothes she wore—salmon colored capris that tied at the knees, a curve hugging tee-shirt with deep 'v' plunging between her breasts, and slip-on clogs. His eyes lingered for a bare moment more on her hair which had been cut, shaped toward her face and hung free.

"Don't startle me like that!" she scolded.

"Sorry," he mumbled. "You look different."

She raised an eyebrow at him. "Aren't I allowed to look different?"

He gave her a crooked smile. "Of course. That wasn't what I meant."

She sighed. "Lark had the notion to go shopping today, after the funeral."

"I know." He folded a hand under each opposite armpit. He dressed back in his Los Angeles mode: black denim jeans shot with silver and a white tee-shirt with silver lip prints on the front. Some of his hair was braided on each side by his temples. "How was it?" It wasn't asked in any type of curious morbidity, only given out of politeness.

"Horrible," she replied. "Are you going to show Jed's work?"

"I don't know," he said with a shrug. "I don't know if I want to give honor to a man who didn't respect his art and his life."

"I don't think that's up to you to decide what type of character he had."

"The man committed suicide, Penny."

"Yes, I know that. But whatever problems he caused, his mind was darker. Just look at his work, Kiley."

"You want me to do the show."

"I want you to do what you feel is best for the art," she clarified.

He went silent for a moment as he gave her the once-over once again. "I like this look."

She flashed him a quick smile and headed toward him, moving from the doorway farther into the gallery.

"So what brought this change?" he asked.

She shrugged. "People evolve, that's what they do."

He gave her one of those looks that clearly said he didn't believe her, but she changed the subject by pointing to the window being installed. "What happened?"

He looked up, frowned, and couldn't tear his eyes away. "The firemen broke the observation window and came in that way. I didn't even know if you were alive until they opened the door from the inside."

She trained her eyes on him, his jaw flexing and tightening at the memories. "It's all hazy, you know," she murmured. "Like I watched it on a television screen. I remember hearing glass shatter. And I remember hearing you scream my name. But that's all, really. I was in this dark little place that made me feel safe."

He was silent for a moment, then, "Penny."

She waited for him to continue.

"I never want to experience that again, not knowing what I was going to walk into and see."

She took one of his hands, holding it as she looked up. She felt his fingers flex around hers and loved the sensation.

"Are you saying...you care for me?"

He shook his head. "I'm saying I love you."

Her heart stopped beating but in the next second it started racing twice its normal speed. Her eyes grew round and she emitted a slight hiccup as she said, "W-what?"

His thumb traced patterns on her soft skin. "I was so damn jealous of Luci, of thinking that you and he could—"

She covered his lips with a finger. "There's no one else, Kiley. What man could possibly compare to you?"

He kissed her finger and smiled a deadly wicked smile. "Perhaps I could convince you to be my muse."

She thought briefly of the pencil sketch hanging on his wall in Paris of a woman he had loved once. She felt special that she could be his next masterpiece. "Ever since I could remember, I loved the expression art brought out from my soul. The colors, the feelings, the depths...all of it. I always knew my heart was meant for art, but until recently, my soul had been lacking the same." She traced a finger down his cheek. "And I found out what brought it all together for me, connecting my heart and soul." She took a deep breath. "It was when I realized how in love with you I am, Kiley," she whispered.

He seemed frozen for a moment, not blinking, not even breathing. And then, like lightning, he grabbed her arm and pulled her against his body, wrapping her tightly in his arms. "Oh God, Penny, I thought I was dying that night. I saw the blood and my heart stopped beating and when I followed it up and found the door locked to my office I went mad. I kept screaming but you never answered and I thought...I thought you might be dead." He shuddered in her arms until his strength gave out and they sunk together to their knees.

"Kiley," she said, but he placed a finger on her lips, raising his head to stare into her dark eyes.

"I've loved you from the moment I met you, Penny," he admitted in a low tone. "But I waited, to give you time, to get a chance to know me. And unfortunately, you started dating Steve."

"Stu," she corrected.

"Whatever," he dismissed, running a hand over her hair. "And for six months I wanted to shake you until you realized you were mine. The day you told me he broke up with you, I knew my time had come. I wasn't going to wait again and have someone else snatch you up. That first night, that first time, was pure heaven to me. Then you ran away and I plunged through hell again."

"I was confused," she admitted. "Look at it from my point of view."

"So I pressed for you to come live with me when I found out your car needed fixing. I thanked my lucky stars for divine intervention. I thought I had messed it up again by being impatient in the shower." He smiled. "Though I don't regret that moment at all."

She smiled back at him.

After a moment, his smile faded. "I don't ever want to lose you, Penny. I love you. I love you so damn much."

His eyes focused on her mouth and a second later he captured them with his own, kissing her till she gave a small whimper of desire.

"Say you'll marry me," he whispered against her lips.

She pulled back. "Marry? Are you sure?"

He brought her hand up to his lips and kissed her knuckles. The tender look in his eyes just about melted her bones. "Will you, Penny Varlet, do me the honor of becoming my wife?"

She gave a very simple answer.

"Yes."

Epilogue

It took a few weeks for Kiley to completely forgive Jedidiah Yuki for the way he opted out of life, or at least enough to start planning a show around the remaining work. They planned it to be a memorial to the artist instead of the man, and Penny thought that was how it should be.

The gallery had been completed the day before the opening night. Kiley decided on a goth look, complete with lots of pleather, buckles and silver studs, and much to many people's surprise, Penny showed up in a matching outfit. She wore a short leather mini paired with fishnets and heavy clunker shoes, her naturally black hair a perfect foil to Kiley's blond angelic highlights. Jed's work had been a series in the same motif so everything blended. They were featured the next day in the fashion section of several trade papers, hailed as a rousing success. No one could miss the blindingly brilliant diamond sported on her left hand.

Exactly one month later, Kiley and Penny married. They decided against a traditional wedding of tulle, lace and silk and chose a small gathering of just family and close friends. Lark ended up giving Penny a book called "How to Have a Happy Ever After with the Boss."

And if anyone had been surprised by the groom's choice of wedding attire, no one commented, even though it wasn't every day that one married in black leather pants.

THE END

ABOUT THE AUTHOR

Beth read her first romance novel, a Harlequin Presents, when she was twelve and from then on it became the staple in her writing. She grew up in rural Missouri but moved her senior year in high school to Delaware. She married young but her marriage only lasted four years. After her breakup she moved to Los Angeles, California where she met Brian. They have one young son and have recently moved to Louisiana. Her son became the reason that she went back to school and earned her national certification as a surgical technician. Through all this, her love of reading and writing grew stronger year after year. She plans to continue working, raising her son, and writing romances that challenge her and delights her readers. Her website will be coming soon but please feel free to contact her at: bdelene@hotmail.com.

Siren Publishing, Inc.
www.SirenPublishing.com